WHY I DID NOT STAND FOR THE PLEDGE TODAY,

by Becca Silverman.

This morning in class I did not stand up for the pledge because it would not have been right if I did. I did not feel too good about the United States of America, and I felt like showing it. In July my brother Stevie was drafted. We were all very upset in my house, and Stevie cried. He didn't want to go to Vietnam and be a soldier. Stevie is my only brother. He is very nice to me. He is nineteen and plays in a rock band named Caribou. I am very angry at the United States for making him leave, and I didn't want to stand up for the pledge because it would be hippochrissy (is that spelled right?) to do it. That means when you do something you don't believe in. In school you said that the flag represents the government. But I don't like the government now. I know this isn't 500 words yet, but I don't have anything more to say.

Bantam Starfire Books of related interest
Ask your bookseller for the books you have missed

CARIBOU

MEG WOLITZER

BANTAM BOOKS
TORONTO • NEW YORK • LONDON • SYDNEY • AUCKLAND

For Rachel and Linda Pastan

*This low-priced Bantam Book contains
the complete text of the original
hard-cover edition.*
NOT ONE WORD HAS BEEN OMITTED.

RL 5, IL age 11 and up

CARIBOU

*A Bantam Book / published by arrangement with
William Morrow & Co., Inc.*

PRINTING HISTORY

William Morrow edition published January 1985

Bantam edition / March 1986

*Starfire and accompanying logo of a stylized
star are registered trademarks of Bantam Books, Inc.
Registered in U.S. Patent and Trademark Office and elsewhere.*

CARIBOU

PART ONE

CHAPTER 1

My brother Stevie's fate was in black and white. My parents wouldn't let us get a color TV—they said it was too expensive. We all sat in the living room watching some stupid comedy show and waiting for the lottery to begin. All the lights were off, and the room looked kind of blue, like we were a family under the sea.

Dad sat in his recliner, leaning back like he was at the dentist's. Mom sat on the edge of the couch, as if she thought the phone would ring at any minute. Stevie was lying on the floor in front of the TV, his long legs stretched out. Me, I sat right next to him, Indian style.

I think you can learn a lot about people from the way they sit. Stevie's foot was jiggling up and down. Dad lifted his arm and squinted at his watch. Mom leaped up from the couch and hurried into the kitchen. I heard the cabinet slam. She came back carrying a tray of Yodels and two glasses of milk. "Here," she said. "Dessert, kids. I almost forgot."

Stevie unpeeled the silver foil, then put the whole Yodel into his mouth.

"You don't have to wolf it down," said Dad, but his voice was soft.

On TV a lady was getting caught in a revolving door. She kept getting flung out real fast, her eyes crossed, and then she'd stagger back and try it again. The audience laughed and laughed.

In our house nobody laughed. We were too nervous. We just sat quietly in the dark living room, waiting. I ate my Yodel, but I wasn't hungry. I don't even remember swallowing.

Finally the show ended. There were a couple of commercials for dog food and deodorant, and then the screen went blank. "This is it," Stevie said in a whisper. I sat up straight, my glass of milk between my hands.

It was a hot summer night in 1970, and I had just come home from a month at summer camp. We were waiting to see if my brother Stevie would have to go fight in the Vietnam War. On TV a man was going to pick birthdays from a big barrel and read them out loud. If your birthday was one of the first ones picked, you were in big trouble. "The chances of your date coming up early are really slim," everybody told Stevie. "Relax. There are three hundred and sixty-five possibilities."

Stevie was born on July 9, in the middle of a heat wave. Mom went into labor, and Dad couldn't get the car started. Stevie was born on a lawn chair in the garage.

He likes to tell that story. "I remember it very clearly," he insists, although it can't be true. You can't really remember the day you were born, can you?

A picture flickered onto the TV screen. A very serious-looking bald guy stood there, next to a big barrel that kept whirling around. It was like the bingo tumbler at the local church. Once I went with my friend Janette's family and I won $25.

But inside this barrel there were only dates, no letters to spell out anything. All around the country, nineteen-year-old boys sat in front of TV sets, crossing their fingers. "Okay," Stevie said to the bald man on TV. "Just hurry up, you old geezer. Say a date, any date. But do not say July ninth; save it until last. I repeat, *do not* say July ninth."

The man on TV cleared his throat. He was wearing a gray suit. Maybe it was some other color, but of course I couldn't tell. Everything on the set looked gray. The pieces of paper in the barrel whirled around. The man stuck his arm inside and pulled out the first date. He held it up to his face, real close, as though he were nearsighted. Then he looked straight into my brother

Stevie's eyes and almost seemed to smile. "July ninth," he said. "July ninth."

I froze there on the floor. We all froze, like we wer having our family picture taken. In that one secon everything changed. Just because my brother was bor on a particular day during a heat wave a long time ago

"Oh, my God," said Mom. I turned around and looke at her. She was leaning back against the pillows. I looke at Dad; he hadn't moved. I looked at Stevie. He wa shaking his head.

"I don't believe this," he said. He sprang to his fee "Mom, Dad!" he said. "What am I going to do?" An then my brother Stevie burst into tears.

The last time I had seen him cry was six years ea lier, when he was thirteen and I was six, and our colli Skipper got hit by a car. That day he had stood in th road, holding Skipper in his arms. Dad had finally com out and brought him in. Skipper was okay; he just ha a broken leg.

But now nobody went over to Stevie. Nobody touche him, patted him on the shoulder, said it was okay. Be cause it wasn't okay.

Stevie just stood there in the middle of the room. H ran his hands through his hair. His voice came ou hoarse, like he had a sore throat. "I didn't think thi would happen," he said. "This is terrible."

I just sat there at his feet. I didn't know what I coul say to make him feel any better. I was only his kid sis ter, Becca the brat. But I didn't have to say anything. A that moment the phone rang, and it kept on ringing. I guessed that it was some relative who had seen the broadcast and knew. Everybody knew.

That was how it all began. Stevie paced around the house that night. Finally he said he was going for a bike ride. I watched from the screen door as he wheeled his ten-speeder out onto the curb and then climbed on. In a second he was gone. I watched his headlight leading the way down the dark street.

"Becca, it's getting late," Mom said to me. "I know you're upset, honey, but you'd better try and get some sleep."

She put her hand on my shoulder, and I looked at her. She had been crying, but now she wasn't any longer. She just looked very tired. I always got scared when I saw Mom cry. She wasn't supposed to cry—she was my *mother*. She cried pretty easily. I remember when we went to see *Gone with the Wind*. She cried so much that the people in the row in front of us kept turning around and saying, "Do you *mind*?"

"Okay," I said to her. "I'll go to bed."

She kissed me on the forehead. Then she went into her bedroom and closed the door. I could hear her and Dad whispering.

I went into my room and closed the door, too. My bedroom was my favorite place to escape to. I could go inside and forget about everything, blot everything out. That's just what I tried to do after the lottery because it upset me too much. I didn't want to think about it. I didn't want to think about anything at all.

A couple of years before, I did some weird stuff to my room, and it looked pretty neat. Mom and Dad let me paint pictures right on the walls. So when I went into my bedroom at night, it was like being in a tropical jungle. There were trees on the walls and pictures of birds and even an elephant, though I didn't make his trunk long enough, so he looked more like a rhinoceros.

Every time I brought friends home from school for the first time, they always said, "Wow," when they saw my room, and I felt happy. That was what happened when I brought Kate home. She had just moved into the neighborhood and sat next to me in my fifth-grade class. We were deskmates, and she was so shy those first couple of weeks that I thought something was wrong with her. I never thought we'd end up friends. I invited her home only because we had to do a project together. It was on the Incas.

We walked into my room. "This is it," I said.

Kate looked around. "Wow!" she said. "This is the greatest room I've ever seen!" That was the longest sentence I'd ever heard her say.

"You really like it?" I asked.

"It's fantastic," she said. "Where did you find someone to paint it?"

"Well, I painted it," I said, blushing a little.

Kate was very impressed. "Do you want to be an artist?" she asked. "I mean, you already *are* an artist! But is it what you want to do when you grow up?"

"Yes," I said. "More than anything."

We forgot completely about the Incas that day. We just talked about being an artist and then about being a doctor, which is what Kate wanted to be. She was very good in science, and she promised to help me study for the next quiz. We suddenly became best friends; it happened that afternoon.

Kate had the best hair of any girl in school. It was very long—down her back—and she usually wore it in a braid. When she let it loose, she looked like a girl on a shampoo commercial.

"You have the neatest hair," I said.

"It's a real pain to wash it," she said. "It takes a year. My mother and father tell me I'm wasting water."

We sat facing each other on the bed, surrounded by the creatures in my jungle. We listened to a Beatles record. We talked about which Beatle we liked best. We liked different ones, so it was okay. She liked George, and I liked John. We wondered if we would ever get to meet the Beatles.

"By the time we're old enough to be taken seriously by them they'll already be old," she said.

The boys in school weren't exactly like the Beatles. Mostly they were jerky and pretended to be grossed out every time you went near them. There was only one who was nice. His name was Mitchell Sampson, and sometimes he said hello to me, and sometimes he didn't. It depended on what kind of mood he was in. He just had a lot of thoughts inside his head, I guess. He was always making inventions that didn't work. He made strange little machines out of string and batteries and Popsicle sticks. Kate and I both agreed that Mitchell Sampson was the nicest boy in school.

"You're so shy in class," I said. "How come?"

She smiled. "I hardly know anybody," she said. "And the class is so big. Where I used to live, I went to a tiny school with only five kids in my class."

"Five kids!" I said. "I can't believe it! You could never pass notes or anything because everybody would see."

"*Everything* was different," Kate said. "We didn't have any grades. We didn't even have desks. Just beanbag chairs. And we called the teachers by their first names. My teacher's name was Willow."

I tried to imagine a school like that, but I couldn't. Kate said she used to live in the woods. Her house was made out of glass and pine. Then her father got transferred to another job. He taught college, and now the Ruskins lived in a split-level three blocks away from me. I was glad she lived so close.

From that day on, whenever I had a problem or was just bored, I'd run over to Kate's house. I loved it there. It was filled with plants and books in orange crates, and you were allowed to put your feet up on the couch. Her mother and father were pretty young. Both of them were short and looked alike. There is a cartoonist who draws people who look like the Ruskins—all fuzzy and friendly and kind of round.

The night of the Vietnam lottery it was too late for me to go over to Kate's house. I just sat alone in my room, but the paintings on the walls didn't make me feel much better. They just made me feel closed in. I imagined that there were soldiers hiding in the leaves.

I would get to see Kate the next morning, and we would talk. She would understand everything because that's just the way she was. Finally, thinking about talking to Kate, I fell asleep. I didn't even remember to take off my clothes. I woke up in the morning in my jeans and rumpled T-shirt.

Kate and I met every day on the corner of Carla Drive and Joanne Street and headed for the town pool. All the streets in my neighborhood were named after girls. They were the names of the women in the builder's family. I wished our street had a nice name, like Greenwood Circle or Riverfront Road. Instead, we lived at 15 Marsha Lane.

Kate came down the street, swinging her towel. "Hi," she said. She took a close look at me and knew something was wrong. "What's up, Becca?" she asked, and then she remembered. "Oh, the *lottery*," she said. Her family didn't have a TV.

I nodded. "Stevie's birthday was picked first. That means he's almost definitely going to be drafted. He has to go for a physical. He'll have to go to Vietnam."

"That's awful," Kate said. "That's the worst thing." Kate would never admit it, but I think she had a crush on my brother. He was always pretty nice to my friends. He never talked to them like they were idiots. And he remembered their names.

We walked along together. Kate's braid bounced

against her back. "He's the only brother I have," I said. "I don't want him to go to Vietnam." My eyes filled with tears.

My family had never talked about what we would do if Stevie got drafted. I guess none of us believed it really *would* happen.

Stevie has been pretty good to me most of the time. When I was little, he ignored me a lot, but then things changed. He got nicer. I'm not sure when or why it happened. He just started offering to help me with schoolwork and to fix my bicycle chain when it broke. We started to play together, even though we were years apart in age.

We pretended that we had a television show called *The Silverman Kids' Fun Hour*. We would run into the living room from the hallway, like we were running out onto a stage, and thousands of people in the audience were cheering. It was like *The Ed Sullivan Show*, but we played all the parts.

"Hi, everybody!" Stevie would say. "I'm Stevie."

"And I'm Becca!" I would pipe in.

"And we're the Silverman Kids!" we would say together.

"Today we have a great show for you," Stevie would say. "Let's open it with the greatest rock group in the world. Fresh off the boat from England—Stevie and the Shake-a-Puddins!"

And then he would pretend to be playing an electric guitar. He would close his eyes and let his mouth drop open and look like he was in pain. He would make twanging sounds as he plucked the strings of his invisible guitar. Then I would come onstage and do a cartwheel, the only thing I knew how to do. And then Mom would call us in to help set the table.

We finally got too old for this game. But Stevie still wanted to be a rock star. He and a couple of friends started a real rock band. They called themselves Caribou. Stevie graduated from high school and decided to hang around the house, playing with the band and working at the Dairy Queen.

Stevie was the lead singer and guitarist of Caribou. The band practiced every weekend in the garage where Stevie was born, and they were getting better and better. They had already played a couple of bar mitzvahs and three graduations last spring. Stevie sat up late into the night, writing songs for the band to play. Sometimes I could hear him as he sang to himself in his bedroom. His voice was very soft and a little rough.

I swam for a long time the morning after the lottery. I stayed in the water until my fingers wrinkled up and my lips started to turn blue. "Are you *ever* coming out?" Kate shouted from the side. But it felt good to swim; it helped me forget about everything.

That's pretty much the way I got through the rest of the summer. I swam all the time and lay out in the sun. Freckles popped up all over my face. At home we avoided the subject of Vietnam. We would just have to wait until Stevie's physical and see what happened. But I knew he would have to go; he was in perfect shape.

Finally the summer came to an end, and it was time to start school again. This year didn't look too promising, and it was all because of one thing: Miss Brodskey. She was known as the teacher with no sense of humor. It wasn't that she was mean. It was just that she never smiled and never understood jokes. When other teachers had parties on the day before Christmas vacation, Miss Brodskey's class had Quiet Time. I wasn't looking forward to school this year. The only good thing was that Kate and I were in the same class again.

On the first day Kate and I lined up in the schoolyard with everyone else. I started to talk with a couple of kids I hadn't seen all summer, but then the bell rang, and we all shuffled in through the doors. There was the usual first-day-of-school stuff to be done; we went around the room and said our names, so that Miss Brodskey would know who we were. Then there was seat assignment, and by some miracle I got to sit right next to Kate again! After that we did current events.

"As most of you know," said Miss Brodskey, "this summer there was a draft lottery. How many of you happened to watch it on television?"

About half of the kids raised their hands.

"I'd rather watch *Laugh-In*," said Tommy Vesco.

"Well," said Miss Brodskey, "I think it's important for all of us to know what's going on in the world we live in. A lot of young men will be going off to fight in the war now. Some of them may be people you know."

People I know very well, I thought. I had been trying not to think about it all summer, but now everything flooded back to me, and I felt terrible. *Stevie was really being drafted.* Kate threw me a sympathetic look. But I couldn't think about it for too long because all of a sudden Miss Brodskey announced that we were going to have a surprise quiz in math, to see how much we had remembered over the summer.

Ellen Harrison passed out the dittos, and when she placed one on my desk, I held it up to my nose and inhaled deeply. I like the smell of fresh ink. It's almost as good as the smell of cookies baking. I knew that I was going to flunk this test, but it didn't really matter to me. I had more important things to worry about.

CHAPTER 2

ON A SATURDAY MORNING IN EARLY WINTER STEVIE
went for his army physical. "I'll be fine, Mom," I heard
him say, shrugging away from my mother, who wanted
him to eat something before he left.

"You need your breakfast," she said as he slammed
out of the house. "Well, at least I know that *you'll* eat
breakfast, Becca," she said to me, and then we went into
the kitchen together.

I sat at the table while Mom poured an oval of pan-
cake batter onto the griddle. It hissed and sputtered, and
she flipped it over perfectly. Mom didn't go to work; she

took care of the house and cooked. Her best friend was Mrs. Klein, and they talked on the phone every day. They played cards once in a while, too.

In the summertime, when we all went to the public pool, Mom and Mrs. Klein and a couple of other ladies sat around a table and played Mah-Jongg. I didn't understand how to play the game. There were all these pretty tiles with pictures on them. I swam all day, and Mom never went in the water. One time I actually convinced her to go in.

"Well, just this once," she said, and then she put a bathing cap on her head and strapped it under her chin like a motorcycle helmet. There were big rubber flowers on the bathing cap. She swam one lap, her head above the water the whole time.

When I swim, I like to be a fish. I go deep under the water, scraping my hands along the bottom of the pool. I can swim very far like that without ever coming up for air.

But now the pool was closed until next summer. Mom and Mrs. Klein and two other friends played bridge instead of Mah-Jongg. But mostly Mom stayed home and cooked a lot. I think it made her feel better.

Now she was squeezing orange juice. We had one of those old-fashioned squeezers made out of heavy metal. You put half an orange in and press down really hard, and the juice comes out of a little spout.

"Herb, breakfast is ready!" Mom called, and my dad came in from the bedroom.

"Morning," he said to me, his head still in the newspaper. We ate together. Mom never sat down; she just hovered above us, refilling our plates. It always made me nervous when she did this. I rarely ever saw her eat. All during meals she was always standing at the stove or the sink.

"Steven left without breakfast," Mom said.

"Oh?" said Dad. He put down his newspaper and took a drink of coffee. "He's nineteen now, Harriet," he said. "If he's old enough to fight for his country, he's old enough to decide whether or not he wants to eat breakfast."

Mom didn't say anything. She started washing out the orange juice squeezer. When she shut off the water, Dad started talking again. "You know," he said, "there's such a gloom over this house lately. It's not the end of the world."

Mom and I looked at Dad. "I admit that I was shocked when Steven got picked like that," he said, "but I've been thinking about it, and I think we have to make the best of the situation." He took another sip of coffee. "It's a very serious war there," he said. "Stevie will be going to help put an *end* to it. He'll be fighting for a good cause. It's something to be proud of. I remember when I went off to fight," he said. "I remember the way I felt when I put on my uniform for the first time."

There was a photograph over the fireplace of Dad in his army uniform. He looked very handsome and young. He was a lot thinner then, almost skinny, in fact. The

sleeves of his uniform were just a little too short. His
wrists stuck out at the ends.

There was another photograph next to it, and it was
a picture of Mom. She was what they called a WAC; she
was in the army, too, and had her own uniform with a
skirt instead of pants. The army was where Mom and
Dad met in the first place. There was a big dance, and
Dad was standing against the wall by the punch bowl.
He was very shy and kept drinking cups of punch so he
wouldn't have to ask anybody to dance. But then he saw
Mom, and she was so pretty that he dropped the ladle
back into the bowl and walked right over to her. They
danced all night without stopping. They both had their
uniforms on. They knew right away that they were in
love. I wondered if it's always like that.

Stevie came home late in the afternoon, close to dinnertime. Mom and Dad were sitting in the living room.
I was sitting in the hallway, drawing. I liked the way
the hallway looked at that time of day. The sun would
be just going down, and everything was very peaceful.
I was trying to get it to look right but wasn't having much
luck. I'm better at drawing animals.

I heard the car pull into the driveway, and then the
door banged. Mom and Dad both looked up. Stevie came
into the house. He stood in the doorway, just waiting
there as if he wanted to say something, but then he
changed his mind. He turned and raced up the stairs.

I knew that I had to go talk to him. I put down my
pad and charcoal and went upstairs, too. His door was

closed, and I knocked. "Can I come in?" I asked.

There was a pause, and then Stevie said okay. His room was very different from mine. It was kind of bare and neat, even though everyone says boys are so sloppy. He made his bed every day, unlike me, who hated to make my bed more than anything. Stevie was sitting on the edge of his bed. "Hi, Becca," he said.

"Can I sit down?" I asked, and he nodded. I sat down at his desk, in the swivel chair I liked so much. Even Stevie's desk was neat. All his pencils and pens were standing in an orange can. There was a picture tacked to the wall of Stevie's girl friend, Nina Whitty. She was very pretty and blond, and was wearing a bikini in the photograph. She was laughing.

"What happened?" I asked.

"Nothing," he said.

"What do you mean?" I asked.

"I didn't go," said Stevie. "I got there, and I was in the parking lot, and I saw all these guys walking into the building, and I knew I couldn't do it. As soon as they walked in, they were giving everything up. I freaked out. So I went to Burger King for a couple of hours and just sat in a booth."

I was shocked. "What are you going to do now?" I asked.

"Well," he said, "I guess I'm going to have to decide pretty soon. But I'll tell you, Becca, I'm not going to Vietnam. That's for sure."

"Isn't that illegal?" I asked.

"Oh, yes," he said. "I could go to jail. Or I could go live in Canada. They can't arrest you if you go to Canada."

Suddenly I remembered that there were lots of people who got drafted and didn't go. They were called draft dodgers. I had seen them on the news, holding matches to their draft cards. Dad had shut off the TV in disgust.

"But, Stevie," I said, "what will Mom and Dad say?"

"I haven't the faintest idea, Becca," he said. "They'll probably hit the roof. But it's my life, you know? I'm going to tell them everything at dinner. Listen," he said. "Do me a favor. Tell Mom and Dad that I'll be down when dinner's ready but that I'm taking a nap now. Tell them you don't know *anything*, okay?" he said. "I mean, tell them I wouldn't talk about it."

I nodded and left the room, feeling very confused.

That evening at dinner Stevie told them. We were all waiting for him to say something. Mom was standing at the stove, looking very nervous.

"Well," said Stevie, "I didn't go for my physical."

"*What?*" asked Dad. He held a forkful of potatoes. He put the fork down on his plate.

"I said I didn't go," said Stevie. "I decided that I can't go to Vietnam." He looked very pale as he spoke.

There was the longest silence in the world.

Mom put the pan back in the oven and then came and sat down. She was still wearing her oven mitts. It was like a strange pair of boxing gloves. "What's this about, Stevie?" she asked.

"He said he didn't go for his physical," said Dad. "That's what he said. What happened, Stevie? The war ended today and I didn't hear about it?"

"You don't have to be sarcastic, Dad," Stevie said. "I've been talking to Nina about it, and I've just been giving it a lot of thought. I can't go through with it. I can't go fight in this stupid war."

Dad picked up his napkin and patted his mouth. He looked very angry all of a sudden. "I don't know what I taught you," he said. "But you certainly did not get this from me. I didn't teach my children to shirk their responsibilities. It's funny—I never once heard a single peep out of you before, Steven. I didn't see you marching down in Washington with the youth of America. You were too busy fooling around with that girl friend of yours and playing rock music. But when it comes down to your turn to go, all of a sudden you're Mr. Nonviolence."

"Well, it made me rethink a lot of things," Stevie said. "I know I've goofed off a lot. I could have been more responsible, as you say, Dad. But I wasn't, okay? I wasn't. What am I supposed to do about it now? I know I didn't do so great in high school. But now I'm making my own decisions. I'm taking responsibility for my life, like I'm supposed to."

Dad stood up quickly. His chair knocked into the wall. He tossed his napkin to the table. "I think I've heard enough from you for tonight," he said. And then he left the kitchen.

I couldn't believe it. My dad almost never got excited

about anything, except when the car broke down and it cost a lot to fix it. The three of us sat there. Mom shook her head sadly. "You've upset your father," she said to Stevie. "Go in. Talk to him." She nodded in the direction of the living room. I could hear the TV go on, and then the restless flipping of channels.

"No," said Stevie. "I can't. I don't have anything to say to him if he's going to be like that."

Mom put her hands to her face. She still had those mitts on. "I guess you have to make your own decisions, Stevie," she said. "I'm not sure how I feel about it. I guess I agree with your father that it's important to serve your country, but I just don't know . . ." Her voice trailed off.

Stevie sank a little lower in his chair. Then he shrugged. "It's all making me feel crazy," he said. "I don't want to learn how to use a gun. I have enough trouble with the Dairy Queen machine."

Suddenly he looked at his watch. "Jesus, I've got to go," he said. "I'll be late for work." He stood up from the table. "If Dad wants to talk to me," he said, "then let *him* come to *me*. I've got to go." And then he took off.

Mom and I cleaned up the kitchen together, not saying anything. The warm water in the sink felt nice. I put my arms deep into the suds. When we were done, I asked if I could go over to Kate's house. Mom hesitated. "If your father says it's okay," she said. She never made the tiniest decision without asking Dad; it was weird. So I went into the living room, and my father said it was okay. He didn't even look up from the TV when he spoke.

The Ruskins' house was the only place that could possibly make me feel good that night. Their front door was open, and I could hear music coming from inside— something classical. I rang the bell, but nobody heard me, so I just went in. You were allowed to do that at the Ruskins'. Kate's parents were sitting in the den, playing Scrabble. The stereo was blasting; I don't know how they could concentrate with the music so loud.

" 'Franchise,' give me seventeen points!" yelled Mrs. Ruskin.

"Hi!" I called, and they both looked up. Mr. Ruskin lowered the music.

"Hi, Becca," he said. "I didn't hear you come in. Kate's upstairs."

Mr. Ruskin shouted for Kate to come down. She was wearing a Snoopy T-shirt and old jeans. "I was just playing with my chemistry set," she said. "It's starting to smell like rotten eggs upstairs."

"Come join us," Mrs. Ruskin said. "That's enough science for the night, Kate. We have to sleep up there, you know."

We went into the den, and Mrs. Ruskin put the Scrabble set away. "How are you, Becca?" she asked. "Kate's told us that your brother went for his physical today. What happened?"

"He didn't go," I said. "He doesn't want to go to Vietnam. He told my parents at dinner, and my dad was furious."

Mr. Ruskin shook his head. "I just don't understand some families," he said. The Ruskins sat close together. They really did look alike, except Mrs. Ruskin didn't have a beard and mustache, of course. Mr. Ruskin taught college, and Mrs. Ruskin used to, but now she was taking off a couple of years to write a book. It was all about what things were like in the twelfth century. Life was pretty bad then, she said. People were killing each other all the time, like now.

I sat down on a big pillow on the floor. Stuffing was leaking out of the side. We all talked for a while about a lot of things: my mother and father, and school, and the war. It was funny—people's parents were either for or against the war. Nobody was in between. I kept seeing cars with bumper stickers on the back, things like SUPPORT OUR BOYS IN VIETNAM or else WAR IS NOT HEALTHY FOR CHILDREN AND OTHER LIVING THINGS. It was pretty confusing.

I felt jealous of Kate for having the Ruskins as parents. She got to live with them all the time. Just being in their house for five minutes made me feel good.

Finally it was time for me to go. I sighed and stood up. I really hated having to leave. "Good night," I said. "Thanks for everything."

"Good night, Becca," Mrs. Ruskin said.

"Hang in there," said Mr. Ruskin.

I walked slowly home. When I got to our house, my

dad was out front, walking Skipper.

"Hi, Becca," Dad said. "Did you have fun at your friend's?"

"Yes," I said. I stood next to Dad at the curb, and we waited for Skipper to find a good place to pee. It's funny about dogs—they are very choosy about where they go to the bathroom. Skipper always had to sniff the ground until he found the place that smelled just right. Then he would look around, a little embarrassed, and lift his leg. He did it really casually.

"I'm sorry I lost my temper at dinner," Dad said. "But I meant everything I said. I guess I could have said it a little more calmly."

I stood next to my dad, not knowing what to say. I shoved my hands in my pockets. "It's okay," I mumbled.

When Skipper was all done, we walked into the house together. Dad unhooked the leash, and Skipper trotted over to his little bed in the corner of the kitchen. He curled into a doughnut and went right to sleep.

"I guess I'll do the same," Dad said. "Good night, Becca." He hung the leash over the doorknob and walked slowly up the stairs.

CHAPTER 3

Stevie had made up his mind. He and Dad got into a lot more discussions, which ended in arguments. But Stevie's decision was final.

"Well, I'm going to Canada," he announced one night at dinner. Everything seemed to happen at the dinner table lately. This time his girl friend, Nina, was there. We had pulled up an extra chair, and Stevie and Nina were sitting close together.

"Bon voyage," Dad said. I thought that was really mean of him.

"Dad," I said, "you don't have to be so nasty about it."

"I can't change the way I feel," Dad said. "It's Steven's choice. I just hope he doesn't regret it."

"I won't," Stevie said. "It's the only choice for me." He reached out and touched Nina's arm and smiled at her. She blushed.

"Oh, Stevie," she said.

I liked Nina Whitty a lot. She wasn't exactly the most interesting person in the world, but she wasn't fake at all, like some people. My brother used to have a girl friend back in high school who was a cheerleader and who used to try to win everybody in the family over when she came to dinner. "Mrs. Silverman, I just love this lasagne," Marcie would say. "Maybe you'd be able to write the recipe out for me after dinner on an index card?" And once Marcie said to me, "You know, Becca, I saw you doing cartwheels last week on the lawn. When you start junior high in a few years, you should definitely try out for pep squad. I'll be sure to mention your name to Miss Czerski."

And I'd have to say thank-you to her, and she would smile and chatter on throughout dinner. Nina was much better. She only said things when she had something to say. And she worshiped my brother. Especially now. She just looked at him and seemed to fall apart with love.

They had met at the Dairy Queen. They worked the same shift and started joking around with each other. Nina lived with her parents in the next town. She was nineteen, too. She was taking off a year and then going to college. She wanted to earn a little money first.

Stevie loved his job. Every night was like a date. The Dairy Queen didn't do a very good business in the winter, so Stevie and Nina spent a lot of time alone. Whenever you walked into the room, they always looked kind of funny, like they had just been making out and had pulled apart when they heard you coming.

The next night I went to visit Stevie at work. I took my bike and rode out to the Dairy Queen. There was no snow on the ground, and it was safe. I had reflector tape all over my bicycle, so cars could see me. When I got there, there was a group of teenagers standing by the window. I waited until they drove off, and then I walked up to the counter. Stevie and Nina were sitting together and giggling about something. I knocked on the glass. Moths flew around in the yellow light.

"Hey, it's my little sister," Stevie said to me, and he stood up. He was wearing his white paper cap and apron. "What can I give you, Becca?" Stevie asked.

"A double vanilla with hot fudge," I said. "And nuts. The wet kind."

Stevie went over to the ice cream machine and held a plastic cup under the nozzle. Then he lifted the lever, and a funnel of vanilla ice cream slowly inched out. Then he poured on hot fudge from a dipper and sprinkled walnuts over the top. "Here you are," he said, and he handed it to me. The dish was both warm and cold in my hand. Stevie licked a dab of chocolate off his wrist. He leaned back against the metal counter. Nina saw that we wanted to talk. She went into the back of the room over by the freezers and put a book in front of her face.

"How are things at home tonight?" Stevie asked me. "I always figure that big fights go on as soon as I leave for work. And then I feel bad because you get stuck there."

"They're not fighting tonight," I said. "Mom is playing bridge with her friends. Dad is balancing the checkbook."

"Sounds like a barrel of excitement," said Stevie in this really sarcastic voice he sometimes uses.

"Stevie," I suddenly blurted out, "how long are you going to be here? When are you leaving?"

Stevie shrugged. "I don't know," he said. "I think it will have to be pretty soon, Becca. They might try to track me down."

"I don't want you to go," I said. "I'll be all alone. I'll be an only child."

"Hardly," Stevie said. "That's what you might be if I went to Vietnam. This way I'll still be around. Maybe not near you, but we can write. Remember I wrote you letters the first summer you went to Camp Skylark and I stayed home?"

"Yes," I said, "but it's not the same." I put down my ice cream. I felt my throat closing up, like I was about to cry. He would think I was such a baby, just his bratty little kid sister.

"This is the way it has to be," Stevie said. "It's the only thing to do. I could go to jail; that's another possibility. Do you want to come visit me in jail? Do you want to come talk to me during visiting hours through a glass wall?"

And then we both realized that that was exactly what we *were* doing right then. We smiled. "Come around the back," Stevie said, and he went to open the door for me.

I liked spending time at the Dairy Queen. The refrigerators vibrated so much that you could feel it in your feet. "You want to take a handful of sprinkles for the ride home?" Stevie asked me. I nodded, and reached in and grabbed some sprinkles. I dropped them in the pocket of my jacket. I would find them for weeks afterward, clinging to the wool.

"Look," he said. "It's not that bad. I've been talking to a lot of people, trying to set things up. I might be able to spend some time at this house in Montreal. It will be okay."

"Yeah, I guess so," I said, but I didn't believe it. It wasn't just that Stevie was going to be living in another state, like some of my friends' older brothers and sisters, who went to college far away. He was going to be in another country, and the worst part of it was that he wouldn't be allowed to come home.

It was like one of the stories in my *Red Fairy Book*—somebody gets banished from a kingdom forever. "I hate everything," I said. "It doesn't make any sense that you have to leave and can't come back."

"Well, that's the way things are now," he said. "There's nothing I can do about it." He looked at his watch. "It's after nine," he said. "You'd better get back home. You know Mom will start worrying!"

I said good-night to him and to Nina, and then I went back outside. I rode home in the wind, eating the sprinkles from my pocket.

It was the next day in school that I didn't stand up for the Pledge of Allegiance. I hadn't planned it in advance; it just sort of happened. It was Jimmy Byron's turn to be flag monitor. He got up and took the flag out of its holder. He stood in front of the class and held the flag still. Everybody stood up, scraping back their chairs from their desks.

I started to get up but stopped. I couldn't say the pledge—not today. I was angry with the country today. Miss Brodskey looked at me in surprise but stood where she was. Later that morning, when we were all working quietly on maps, she came over to my desk.

"Becca, are you feeling ill today?" she asked. "I noticed that you sat down during the Pledge of Allegiance."

I felt my face get hot. "No," I said. "I'm okay." I continued to draw Australia.

Miss Brodskey still stood there, making a shadow on the page. "Well, is there any particular reason that you decided not to stand up?" she asked me.

"Yes," I said, but I wouldn't look up. I saw out of the corner of my eye that Kate was watching.

"Do you feel like telling me?" Miss Brodskey asked.

"No," I said.

"Well, you don't seem very talkative today," Miss Brodskey said. She put her hands on her hips. "Perhaps you would prefer to write your reason down for me on paper. How about today, right after school? Five hundred words or so." I finally looked up. Like always, Miss Brodskey wasn't smiling.

It was the first time I had ever gotten into trouble. I wasn't a teacher's pet really, but teachers just happened to like me most of the time. I was sort of medium-popular in school. I wasn't in the very cool group made up of Ellen Frankel, Susan Levitt, and Corinne di Angelo, but I wasn't exactly like Maureen Startz, either, who didn't have any friends. She couldn't read very well, and other kids were mean to her. Tommy Vesco once said, "Maureen *Startz* a sentence and never finishes it!" and everybody laughed. The only person who was nice to her was the cafeteria lady.

The year before, I was briefly popular because I drew everyone's caricature at the school fair. But I was pretty quiet most of the time. Not shy, like Kate, but quiet.

During lunch that day a couple of kids came up to me. "I heard what happened this morning," Susan Levitt said. "Do you think you'll be in a lot of trouble?"

"No," I said, but I wasn't sure. Kate and Emma and Janette and I all sat together at the table in the back, where we usually sat. I drank my milk from its little red carton. An orange whizzed across the room. Another food fight. Tommy Vesco as usual.

The cafeteria was very loud that day. It had started to

rain, and the room seemed damp and hot. Everyone was restless. Lunch was macaroni and cheese, which was one of the worst meals. All the trays got returned with the macaroni and cheese still on them, untouched. Me, I just picked off the melted cheese on top, then ate dessert.

Usually when I got home from school, Mom would fix me a snack, and I would go watch TV for a while, or draw, or listen to records with Kate. But today after school I'd be sitting in the classroom, writing 500 words, which seemed like an awful lot.

At the end of the day the bell rang, and everyone gathered their things and left, except me. "Call me as soon as you get home," Kate whispered.

"Okay," I said.

She squeezed my shoulder. "Don't worry about it," she said. "We'll play the *White Album* later, and you'll feel better."

Miss Brodskey sat at her desk, arranging papers. She seemed to forget that I was there. Maybe I could just slip out now, while she wasn't looking, and she'd never remember that she'd told me to stay.

But all of a sudden she looked up and pushed her glasses higher on her nose. "Becca," she said, "you may begin writing." Then she went back to what she was doing.

I took a pencil out of my zippered pencil case and sharpened it in the built-in sharpener. Then I blew off the shavings. I opened my loose-leaf notebook to a clean page. I sat there, not writing anything for a few minutes. One window in the classroom was open. Outside, I could hear a couple of kids yelling.

I wrote at the top of the page, in capital letters, "WHY I DID NOT STAND FOR THE PLEDGE TODAY, by Becca Silverman." Then I put my pencil down.

I didn't know what I could say to Miss Brodskey. There was no way she could understand what I felt. But I would have to give it a try. So this is what I wrote:

This morning in class I did not stand up for the pledge because it would not have been right if I did. I did not feel too good about the United States of America, and I felt like showing it. In July my brother Stevie was drafted. His birthday came up first out of 365 dates. We were all very upset in my house, and Stevie cried. He didn't want to go to Vietnam and be a soldier. But he knew he had to. Then one day Stevie told us that he wasn't going to go fight in the war. He was going to go to Canada instead. It is the government that is making him leave. He is my only brother. He is very nice to me. Sometimes, when I do well on your tests in school, it is because Stevie helped me study. He didn't do too well in school, but he knows how to make studying kind of fun. When we were doing the continents, he taught me tricks to remember them. He said that Africa looked like a lamb chop, and ever since then I've never forgotten that. He made me funny flash cards when we did the multiplication tables in the third grade. There was a riddle on each flash card. If you got the table right, you'd get to turn over the card and find the answer to the riddle. Stevie is nineteen and plays in a rock band named Caribou. He also works at the Dairy Queen. I am very angry at the United States for making him leave, and I didn't want to stand up for the pledge because it would be hippochrissy (is that spelled right?) to do it. That means when you do something you don't believe in. In school you said that the flag represents the government. But I don't like the government now. I know it's better than in some countries, where you can't even go to school, and you never have enough food. I always used to take around a UNICEF box on Halloween, and I'd put in my allowance for the week. I felt bad when we saw that movie about the poor family in Ecuador. I know this isn't 500 words yet, but I don't have anything more to say.

Then I put down my pencil. I figured it was too soon to get up and put the paper on Miss Brodskey's desk. So I just sat there for a little while, listening to the sounds outside. Finally Miss Brodskey looked up. "All finished, Becca?" she asked. I nodded.

"Well, let's see what you've done," she said, and I walked up to her desk and gave her the piece of paper. I stood there while she read it. I thought she was going to get very angry that it wasn't anywhere near 500 words. When she was finished, she put the page down and looked out the window. She didn't say anything. Then finally she turned to me.

"Why didn't you tell me this before?" she asked softly.

I shrugged. I didn't usually tell my teachers what went on at home. Nobody did. And I don't think anybody ever wanted to tell Miss Brodskey anything.

"I'm sorry that things are hard for you right now, Becca," she said.

"That's okay," I said, and I played with a paper clip on her desk.

"Will you help me clean the blackboards?" she asked me.

I was surprised. "Sure," I said.

So we stood there together, me and Miss Brodskey. First we used the erasers. I don't know why they called blackboards blackboards—all of the ones in our school were green, not black. I erased a whole day's work—fractions and long division and then a poem by Emily Dickinson. When we were done, the board was still all smeary, so we sponged it down. I worked very hard, and soon all the chalk dust was gone.

"Thank you, Becca," said Miss Brodskey. "That was very helpful of you. You may go now."

I walked home in the late afternoon. Miss Brodskey wasn't so bad after all—imagine that. She had read what I wrote and thought about it seriously. I thought I would probably stand up for the pledge the next day. Once was enough.

As I went down the street, a big green car drove slowly by. I looked in. It was Miss Brodskey! The car looked old; it had fins on it. Miss Brodskey was going home, too. I wondered where she lived, what she ate for dinner. It was always funny to think about your teacher having real lives.

Once when I was nine, I ran into my fourth-grade teacher, Mrs. Aliano, in the supermarket. It had made me so excited! She was just walking up the aisle wheeling a basket. And sitting in the front of the basket was a little kid. I couldn't believe it! Mrs. Aliano was holding a jumbo box of Wheaties. "Why, hello, Becca," she said when she saw me, and then her kid started gurgling. "Here, Anthony, hold this," she said, and then she gave him the box of cereal to play with.

I had said a very shy hello, and then raced to find my mother. "Mom! Mom!" I screamed. "I just saw Mrs. Aliano and she was buying cereal and she has a kid and everything!"

Mom was at the check-out counter already, handing in coupons. "Oh? That's nice, dear," was all she said, not looking up.

She didn't understand how weird it was to see your teachers outside school. They had a whole life of their own. Even Miss Brodskey did. She probably went home to her house and sat in a chair and graded papers at night, and didn't smile.

But she was okay after all. She could have been really mean to me and sent me to the principal's office. She wasn't a monster, the way some kids said. But I knew that no one else would believe me.

CHAPTER 4

A FEW DAYS LATER MY BROTHER'S BAND WAS GOING TO be playing at a bar mitzvah. It was Jane Lerner's brother's bar mitzvah. A lot of us in the sixth grade were invited because Neil Lerner didn't have too many friends of his own. His sister's friends were only a year younger, so his mother thought it would be a nice idea to invite us.

It was held at a temple near my house. My brother and the band got there early to set up. As I went up the steps of the temple, I saw my brother going around back,

carrying a drum. I had a lot of feelings about that drum.
I had painted the picture on it. Stevie had asked me to,
and I had worked on it for days. It was a painting of deer
antlers. As I think I mentioned, the band's name was
Caribou. That's a kind of reindeer that's going extinct.
There aren't too many of them left in the world. Most of
them live up north. I don't know who thought up the
name for the band, but it was better than some of the
other names they came up with first: the Wet Noodles
or the Lifeguards. The idea was to come up with a name
that didn't really have any importance but just sounded
good. I liked the word "Caribou." It sounded kind of
classy, I thought.

My brother and the bass player, Gary, wrote a lot of
music for Caribou, but when they played bar mitzvahs,
they had to sing a lot of famous songs also. Stevie said
the parents liked that best of all.

First I sat in the temple next to Kate, and the rabbi
spoke for a while, and then Neil came up to the stand.
He was very short. He had a yarmulke on his head, and
he said some things in Hebrew. He spoke like he was
singing, but not quite. Every couple of words you could
hear a tune, and then it would stop and come back again.
It felt nice to sit in the cool red room. There was a lot
of wood and carpeting. Everyone was dressed up. I got
to wear my favorite party dress. It had bluebirds all over
the front.

After the ceremony we all went into another room,
where my brother and his band were. There was lunch

first, and dessert, and then I handed Neil his present, which was a silver pen and pencil set. Mom had picked it out for me.

Then all of a sudden my brother was up on the platform, warming up. He strapped his electric guitar around his shoulder and played softly. Gary and Peter came onto the platform, too, and adjusted the microphones.

Then they were ready. "One, two, three, four . . ." Stevie said, and Caribou started playing.

"Come on, baby, light my fire," Stevie sang.

A couple of kids got up to dance. The band was a hit! Stevie's voice sounded wonderful—really old and deep. Not the way it sounded at night, when he sang to himself in his room. That was nice, too, but different. I wasn't sure which one I liked better.

"Your brother's fantastic," Jane said to me.

"Well, your brother read that Hebrew stuff really well," I said, but she knew it wasn't the same.

A couple of grown-ups got up to dance. There was a lady who looked pretty old, but she was wearing a minidress and big spiral earrings. She had tall hair. She danced with a man in a light blue suit. I guessed that they were somebody's aunt and uncle. The dance floor got crowded all of a sudden. I was just sitting at the table with Kate when I heard a voice next to me.

"Do you want to dance?" it said.

I looked up. Mitchell Sampson was standing there. His hair was combed back out of his face, and I could see his eyes for the first time ever. They were pale gray.

"Well, okay," I said, and Kate kicked me lightly under the table. We would talk about Mitchell later. I was led out onto the dance floor. Stevie was singing a medley of Beatles songs. Mitchell wasn't the greatest dancer in the world, but then again, neither was I. We both danced kind of stiffly, not moving too much. All of a sudden Stevie started singing "Norwegian Wood," and I wasn't sure what I was supposed to do. You had to slow dance or else sit down. Most of the other kids sat down.

Mitchell looked at me, and we both smirked. "You want to?" he asked.

"All right," I said. He put his arm around me, and I put my arm on his back. He smelled nice, like spice or something. He didn't step on my feet at all, the way you always hear boys do. He talked to me a little bit, telling me about an invention he was working on. It was something that would actually flip over a record on the stereo, so you wouldn't have to get up and do it yourself. It would be in the shape of a giant hand.

We sat down at the end of the song, and Mitchell went back to where he was sitting across the room. "Did we look okay?" I asked Kate.

"You looked great," she said. "Like you really belonged together."

I felt happy. I watched Mitchell eat a piece of ice cream cake. Then I watched my brother for a while. Stevie had a bandanna around his head, and his hair curled out at the sides. He smiled at some of the girls when he sang.

At the end of the bar mitzvah everyone got a box of

candy to take home. Kate and I opened ours in the car. My dad was driving. I handed him a chocolate buttercream, and he ate it while he drove.

"I'll talk to you later on the phone," Kate said when we dropped her off. "Thanks, Mr. Silverman."

She went into her house and waved from the door. I felt another streak of jealousy then. It was a cold, snowy afternoon, and the Ruskins were probably building a fire in their fireplace and sitting around it with books.

I had never been jealous of Kate until this thing happened with Stevie. It just wasn't fun to be at home anymore. Everyone was tense and raised their voices a lot. I started spending more time in my room. I lay on my bed and listened to the Beatles.

Stevie came home a little while later. He knocked on the door of my room. It was usually me who had to go knock on his door. He poked his head in. "Come on in," I said. "You were great! Everybody said so."

"Thanks," he said. "I think it went okay. It was even kind of fun, especially at the end, when the grandparents got up to dance together. That was real nice."

Stevie stood in the middle of my room and looked at the walls. "I love these paintings," he said. "I hope you don't stop, Becca."

"I'm never going to stop," I said.

"You'll get your own show at the Museum of Modern Art in a couple of years," he said, "and I'll come to the opening and tell everybody I'm your brother, and they won't believe me."

I laughed, but I had a terrible thought: What if I did get famous one day and have an art show, and they didn't let Stevie back into the country to see it, even just for one day? What if they never let him back in again?

He went over to the wall and ran his hand along the neck of a giraffe I had painted.

"Stevie," I said, "promise me that you won't leave without telling me first."

"Of course," he said. "I wouldn't do something like that. Don't worry about it." He paused. "But you know," he said, "I think I'm going to have to take off pretty soon."

How soon? I thought, getting panicky. Tomorrow? Tonight? Would he wake me with a suitcase in his hand and tell me he was going? Would I get up the next day and find all his things gone from his room?

"Stevie," I said, "I didn't stand up for the pledge the other day. It was because of you."

"What do you mean?" he asked.

"I decided that I didn't want to pledge allegiance to the flag," I said. "Not while they're making you leave the country."

He smiled. "I appreciate it, Becca," he said. "But you don't have to do that for me."

"Well, I just did it once," I said. "But I may do it again. It depends on how brave I'm feeling."

"Aren't you going to get into trouble?" he asked me.

"Miss Brodskey was angry," I said, "but then she had me write an essay, and I wrote all about you. She seemed to understand."

"A lot of kids in high school didn't stand up for the

pledge," Stevie said. "They were always getting into hassles with the homeroom teacher. But they didn't decide not to stand up because somebody had to go off to Canada. They did it because of the war. That seems to make more sense, don't you think?"

"Yeah," I said. "I guess so." I felt very dumb. I wanted Stevie to be impressed.

"Look, I think it's great that you're taking an interest like this," he said. "Most kids don't. I didn't."

"I just get fed up," I said. "All I'm supposed to do every day is concentrate on my homework and get good grades. But I can't pretend that all this other stuff isn't going on right in the house."

"You want to get involved?" Stevie asked. I nodded. "Then you've got to find your own way of doing it," he said. "For me, it means going to Canada. But it's got to be something different for you, Becca. You really have to think it out. That's what I did when I got drafted. I went and thought about it a lot. I must have ridden my bike up and down every street in the whole town."

I lay in bed a long time that night before I fell asleep. It was still a little bit light in my room because of the street lamp in front of the house. I could see the animals I had painted. They looked like they wanted to burst out of the walls and come into my room.

I remembered the summer I painted them. I was sick with the mumps, and my neck was like a bag of potatoes. I had nothing to do and was very bored. I stayed inside all day, drinking juice and reading *Cherry Ames, Flight Nurse*. Dad wheeled the TV set into my room, and

I watched *Jeopardy!* I got pretty good at it. Sometimes Mom or Dad or Stevie would come into the room and watch with me and try to answer the questions. In the afternoon Mom and I would watch soap operas together.

"Oh, she's nothing but trouble," Mom said about one of the characters. "She's going to marry that nice Dr. Foster, and watch out." And sure enough, everything that Mom predicted always happened.

While everyone else was outside swimming or going to camp or playing softball, I was lying in bed, looking at the white walls. I complained to Mom that it was so dull staring at the same thing every day.

"You're imaginative," she said. "Why don't you do something interesting with your walls?"

I couldn't believe she said that. The next day she bought me a whole bunch of cans of paint, and brushes, and let me alone in the room. I worked for days and wouldn't let anybody see. I made Mom leave my breakfast tray outside my door, instead of coming in. Finally I was done with an entire wall, and I let my family in. They all crowded into the doorway.

"Well," Dad said, "I've got to hand it to you, Becca. That certainly looks beautiful." And Dad almost never gave compliments. Everybody raved about it, and then I covered the other three walls with animals and plants, too. When I was finished, the room was really beautiful. It was like stepping into a building at the world's fair. The wildlife pavilion maybe.

It was funny—I don't know where I got my ideas from. I didn't use an encyclopedia to copy pictures out of. The pictures were just there in my head. Maybe it was because of all those class trips to the Bronx Zoo when I was little. I was always last on line at the bus when it was time to leave. There would be a buddy count, and I would be missing. I could usually be found standing in front of the lion's cage or over by the peacocks. Once in a while one of the peacocks would decide to show off his big tail. It was amazing, with about 100 colors in it, like a Crayola box. I never forgot the way it looked.

Miss Brodskey wasn't too big on class trips. She said that she thought there was enough to learn right in the classroom without having to pay extra money to go somewhere else. One day at lunch a couple of kids started making fun of Miss Brodskey. "I bet she was around in the Stone Age," said Janette.

"Yeah, and she scared off the dinosaurs," said Corinne.

I felt bad for Miss Brodskey, so I stuck up for her. "She's okay," I said, but nobody seemed to hear.

On Friday night the next week I asked Kate if she wanted to sleep over. We had never done that before. "Okay," she said. "I'll come over after dinner."

When she arrived, we put on some records and listened to them for a while, and then we made popcorn in the kitchen. "You girls don't stay up too late," Mom said. "You'll make yourselves sick."

Kate and I went into my room and jumped on the bed.

"We're too old to jump on beds!" Kate said, but she didn't stop.

"And are we too old to throw pillows?" I asked, and whacked her softly in the stomach with my pillow.

She shrieked and hit me back with hers. We both laughed, and Mom banged on the wall. Kate and I stayed up very late, talking about everything.

"Becca?" she asked when we were about to go to sleep.

"Yeah?"

"Do you think boys will ever love us?"

I thought about this for a minute. "Well, I guess so," I said. "There's no reason that they won't. We're both okay-looking, especially you with that hair. And we're smart and do well in school."

"I don't think that those are the things that really matter," Kate said.

"What do you mean?" I asked. I turned over on my elbow so I was facing her. She was lying in a sleeping bag on the floor.

"Oh, I don't know," she said. "I guess maybe I think it's something spiritual. Like they fall in love with your soul."

"Where did you hear this?" I asked.

"I read it in a book," she said. "It was on my parents' bookshelf. It was all about love. I didn't understand a lot of it."

"Have you ever loved a boy?" I asked her. "In your old school in Vermont? Were any of the other five kids boys at least?"

"Yeah, two of them," she said. "I liked one a lot. His name was Derek. Sometimes I have daydreams that I'm grown-up and married to him, and we're both doctors and we do husband-and-wife surgery. You know, side by side."

I laughed. "Maybe I'll marry a painter," I said. "And I'll paint a picture of a head, and he'll fill in the eyes and nose and mouth."

"My parents do a lot of things together," Kate said.

"I noticed," I said. "I think it's great. My parents hardly *talk* anymore, ever since the lottery. Dad stays up late watching TV, and in the morning he leaves for work early. Mom plays cards a lot. I have nothing to say to them. That's why I like being at your house so much."

"You only see the good parts of my parents," said Kate. "But there are other times when I might as well be invisible as far as they're concerned."

"Well," I said, "I always have a great time at your house. It's a lot friendlier over there."

"It's pretty nice here," said Kate. "Right here. Just staying up and talking. Especially in this room with all your paintings on the walls. I always wondered what it felt like to sleep in here, surrounded by all the animals."

"Well, how *does* it feel?" I asked her.

"Safe," she said. "Nice and safe." And with that we both fell fast asleep.

CHAPTER 5

My BROTHER LEFT THE COUNTRY ON A SUNDAY MORN-
ing in February. I watched him pack all day Saturday—
stood in the doorway of his room as he filled a duffel
bag with odds and ends. His steamer trunk lay open on
the floor, pants and shirts folded neatly inside. It was
the same trunk that Stevie had taken to Camp Skylark
for seven years in a row.

The first time I went to Camp Skylark, I was very
homesick. I sat on the top of my bunk bed and swung
my legs out into the air and cried. My parents had sent
me a letter with a picture of Skipper begging. On the

back of the photograph, my mom had written the words "I miss you, Becca. Arf! Arf! Love, Skipper." Then she had drawn a little paw print, as though Skipper had signed it.

The camp was way up in the mountains. The air felt different there. Sometimes, walking along the nature trail, I would suddenly get very dizzy. Stevie's cabin was all the way on the other side of the woods, in the boys' division. We swam a lot and had arts and crafts, and I had the nicest counselor in the world. Her name was Jessie Diggory, and she was tall and red-haired and looked like a pony when she ran. She went to college during the year, and she was studying psychology. Sometimes she gave us psychological tests at night. She would pass out pieces of paper and ask us to draw a house and then a man and a woman. We would sit on our beds and draw and show her what we had done. Jessie would stay up late with us, telling us what our drawings meant.

I loved to be with her. We had a cookout on the beach one night, and we roasted potatoes in tinfoil and then had s'mores. We drank bug juice from a thermos, and I had brought along my collapsible cup, which was a big hit since none of the other kids had ever seen one before.

Jessie had brought along her guitar, and she played songs and taught us the words. She taught us a song called "Where Have All the Flowers Gone?" and for some reason it made me cry.

After the song, when everyone was just sort of sitting around the fire talking, Jessie came over and sat next to me. It was cold right there by the water. She sat down on a piece of driftwood and zipped her sweat shirt up to her chin. "You look a little teary tonight, Becca," she said.

"Well, I was just thinking about my dog," I said. "I started thinking about him during the song. It made me very sad."

"What's your dog's name?" Jessie asked me.

"Skipper," I said. "He's just a pup—a collie pup—and we're teaching him tricks."

"I have a dog, too," Jessie said. "I mean, he lives at my parents' house in Cleveland, but I see him when I go home for vacations. His name is Goofy."

I looked at Jessie. Her hair looked even brighter red in the firelight. I wondered if I would be like her when I was her age, if people would look up to me like that. She was good at everything: singing and sports, especially archery, and arts and crafts. We pasted shell macaroni on boxes and spray-painted them gold. Then we gave them to our mothers to use as jewelry boxes, but they never did. Jessie was always very kind and never yelled at us to clean up, the way another counselor did that summer. Everybody hated that counselor. She was mean and little and left in the middle of the summer, saying the mosquitoes were eating her alive. But Jessie never complained, and the mosquitoes seemed to ignore her. We all walked around scratching the bites on our elbows and knees, but Jessie never got bitten once. She had a boyfriend in college whose name was Zack, and she showed us his picture. We all passed it around solemnly. He wasn't very handsome, but you could tell that he was extremely intelligent and sensitive. We just knew that they were right for each other.

"Do you think your parents will bring Skipper up on visiting day?" Jessie asked me.

It was a great idea; it hadn't even occurred to me! "Maybe," I said. "I'll write them tomorrow and ask. That would be fantastic."

Jessie smiled. "It's very nice having you in my cabin this year, Becca," she said. "You're a good camper."

I could have sat there all night with her, just listening to the water and the other kids talking in the distance. Someone was playing Jessie's guitar, or at least trying to play. Everyone knew it was important to handle the guitar *very carefully* because it belonged to Jessie. Each kid would try to play a couple of chords and then pass it on to the next person. Jessie never minded. She trusted all of us.

I was feeling kind of sleepy, but I liked the dampness of sitting near the water and the way the sand was cold and soft under my bare feet. I was really annoyed when Beverly Madison ran over and interrupted our talk. "Jessie! Jessie!" Beverly called. "Alison skinned her knee!" In the distance I could hear someone whimpering.

"Okay, Beverly," Jessie said, and she stood up. "We'll talk more really soon, Becca," she said, and she smiled at me.

But we never did get to talk again like that. There were

so many kids for Jessie to pay attention to, and my day
were always filled. It seemed that if I wasn't makin
lanyards, I was taking diving lessons or getting strappe
to someone's ankle in a three-legged race.

The end of the summer came, and Stevie and I rod
the bus home together. Our trunks were somewher
down below, in the luggage compartment. Now Stevi
was filling the trunk up once again, taking it much far
ther away than ever before.

I came in and sat down in a corner of his room. Al
the drawers of his bureau were open, and he was emp
tying them out. Every once in a while he would hold u
a T-shirt and say, "Do you want this, Becca?"

I said yes to everything. I held the soft pile of clothin
in my arms, barely looking at it. I just held it agains
me, like it was a stuffed animal or something.

I wished that I could be alone with Stevie on his las
night. I just wanted to sit in his room and have him sin
to me. He had done that a couple of times—let me si
on the edge of his bed while he sang to himself. H
would lean against the headboard and close his eyes an
sing as though he had forgotten I was there. I never go
bored. I could have sat and listened to him for hours.

But tonight, his last night, he wanted to be alone wit
Nina. They would sit in his room and make out, and the
they would both cry a little. They would talk about Nin
coming to visit Stevie in Canada. She would work extr
hours at the Dairy Queen, saving up enough money fo
bus fare.

I wondered if I would ever be able to go visit Stevie. It hadn't even occurred to me before. The idea hit me all of a sudden; if I were a cartoon character, a little light bulb would have appeared over my head. I could go visit Stevie in Montreal if only I could save up the money.

Nina came over for dinner that night. It was a very quiet meal. "The last supper" Stevie called it later. Dad didn't say a word during dinner, at least not until the end. He and Stevie had been giving each other the silent treatment lately.

Nina and Stevie held hands during the meal. It was like they were handcuffed together. Mom kept serving more food; she had made spaghetti and meatballs, Stevie's favorite. He wasn't eating very much of it that night. He sat and twirled his spaghetti on his fork. He looked very depressed.

It was the longest dinner of my life. I could hear the kitchen clock ticking on the wall, and every few seconds there was the sound of silverware scraping against a plate. "I can't take this," I suddenly said.

Everybody looked up.

"Why does it have to be this way?" I asked. "Stevie's *leaving* tomorrow. I don't want the last night to be like this!"

Nobody said anything; they just looked at me. Then Mom shook her head. "You're right, Becca," she said. "We'll try to make it more pleasant." She put on a smile. "How are your parents, Nina?" she asked.

Nina looked startled. Usually nobody asked her any

questions at dinner. "They're okay, Mrs. Silverman," she said. "Dad got a promotion, so things have been pretty good."

Then there was another long silence. Finally Stevie put down his fork and sighed. "Mom," he said, "I can't eat any more. Everything tastes great—you know I love your spaghetti—but I'm just not hungry tonight. Can I be excused?"

Mom started to answer, but Dad cut in. "You can be excused from the table, Steven," he said. "But you can't be excused from your responsibilities as an American citizen."

Stevie sat up in his chair, still holding Nina's hand. "Dad," he said, "please don't start. It's my last night in this house." He stood up suddenly, yanking Nina with him. "We'll be in my room," he said. He turned to Mom. "I'm sorry, Mom," he said. And he and Nina left the room.

I sat there alone with my parents. The table felt very big. Then I realized that I'd better get used to it; this was the way it was going to feel from now on. I would look across the table, and there would be an empty chair facing me. I would reach out my leg to kick Stevie lightly, sharing a joke under the table, but I would only be kicking the legs of his chair.

Everybody lost their appetite. We just pushed our food around on our plates, and finally Mom brought our dishes over to the sink. Dad went into the living room and turned on the TV. At the Ruskins' house Mr. Ruskin helped with the dishes, too. Everybody pitched in, and the work got done quickly. Things never stayed neat for very long, though. Mrs. Ruskin wasn't a clean freak like my mother.

"Mom," I said, "I can clean up by myself if you want."

She smiled. "That's sweet of you, Becca," she said. "But I'll be fine. Just sponge down the table, and then you can go upstairs."

I left Mom in the kitchen and climbed the stairs. I stood outside Stevie's door, which was half-open. I could hear talking.

"But I'm not *going* to date anyone else," Nina said. "I'll probably never look at another boy, Stevie. Don't say that."

"Come here, Nina," Stevie said softly, and then I knew that they were kissing. There was no noise.

I went into my bedroom and shut the door. I put on *Abbey Road* and paced around in circles. I tried to sing harmony to "Here Comes the Sun." Then I shut off the record and went back into the hall, outside Stevie's room. I heard talking again, so this time I knocked.

"Come on in," Stevie called.

I went in and sat at Stevie's desk. It was completely clear. Even Nina's photograph was gone. In its place was a tiny hole where the thumbtack had been stuck in the wall. I ran my hands over the smooth desktop.

"You okay?" Stevie asked me.

I nodded. "What time is your bus tomorrow?" I asked.

"Eight," he said. "Are you going to come?"

"Of course," I said. "Promise to wake me up?"

"Sure," he said.

"I hope you'll still come by the Dairy Queen, Becca," Nina said. You could tell that she had been crying; her eyes were puffy. She and Stevie were sitting on the bed leaning against the wall. They had kicked their shoes off.

"I will," I said, but I didn't know if I really would. I wasn't so sure I'd be in the mood for ice cream anymore.

"Do you think you and Dad will ever become friends again?" I asked my brother.

"I don't know," he said. "If we do, it will be a long time from now. He won't budge. And Mom doesn't seem to know how to help. She's scared of taking a stand, I think."

Stevie plugged in his lava lamp, and we watched the colors swirl around. "Did you already say goodbye to Gary and Peter?" I asked him.

"Yeah, this afternoon," Stevie said. "The end of a promising rock star career."

I was always positive that my brother would become famous. If Caribou ever made it big, Stevie would have been the one to have full-page posters of himself in *Tiger Beat* magazine, with his signature scrawled across the bottom: "Luv to all my fans, Stevie Silverman."

I stayed in Stevie's room for a while, and then conversation stopped. I suddenly realized that Stevie and Nina wanted to be alone. "Well," I said, "good night. If you don't wake me up to go to the bus station in the morning, I'll never speak to you again, Stevie."

"I promise," he said.

"Bye, Nina," I said. "See you."

Then I went right to sleep, but I felt terrible.

The next thing I knew, my brother was standing over me, shaking me awake. "Rise and shine, Becca," he said. "Rise and shine."

"Is it time?" I asked in a groggy voice, and he nodded. He was already dressed.

I took a sleepy shower, then came downstairs. Stevie's trunk, duffel bag, and guitar were lined up by the front door. Mom was in the kitchen, opening and closing cabinets. I didn't see Dad. I quickly ate a bowl of dry cereal, then went and waited on the front porch. In a few minutes Stevie pushed through the front door, Skipper trailing him.

"Stay, Skipper," my brother said, and he reached down and bunched up the scruff of Skipper's neck.

Skipper waited in the doorway, standing on his hind legs to look out the glass. His ears were perked up. "Stay, Stevie," I wanted to say to my brother, and maybe it would work and he would go right back inside. But there he was, his duffel bag slung over his shoulder. He made three trips—came back with his trunk and then his guitar. Then my mother was on the porch, her car keys dangling from her hand.

"All ready?" she asked quietly. Stevie said yes.

"Where's Dad?" I asked. "Isn't he coming?"

"No," Mom said.

Stevie stood in the driveway and looked at the house. "Farewell, old house," he said. "Farewell, lawn that I mowed for free all these years."

"Come on already," Mom said, but she was smiling.

It was still kind of gray outside. The grass looked crisp with frost. Down the street a newsboy was bicycling toward us, throwing papers onto driveways. We were about to get into the car when all of a sudden the front door opened. Dad was standing there in his winter coat. I could see his pajama pants sticking out at the bottom.

"Steven," he said.

My brother looked at Mom, then at me. "Just a sec," he said to us, and he walked back to the house.

"Good luck, son," Dad said. "I hope you know what you're doing."

"Yeah, I do, Dad," Stevie said.

"I'm sorry I can't approve of it," Dad said. "I'm not angry, really. Just disappointed. I served my country when I was young, and I still have a lot of feelings about it."

"Yeah, well . . ." Stevie said.

"So, take care of yourself," Dad said, and he reached out to shake Stevie's hand.

Stevie waited a second, but then he shook Dad's hand. It was very formal, like the end of a job interview or something. Dad looked thin and pale in his coat and pajamas, and Stevie looked big and husky in his winter jacket. For the first time I saw how much taller he was than Dad.

Stevie walked back to the car and got in. I slid into the back, and Mom started the engine. Dad still stood on the front porch, watching us drive away. His hands were deep in his pockets.

We didn't say a single word during the drive. Stevie fumbled with the radio and finally put on a pop station with a lot of static. Caribou sounded a lot better, I thought. They could have become stars. I thought about Peter and Gary and wondered if they would continue playing without Stevie. Maybe they would get a new lead singer and guitarist. But how could anybody replace my brother?

And then I had this really strange thought: Maybe my parents would get another son to replace Stevie. I would wake up one day and find this new kid eating breakfast downstairs. Someone my dad would love more.

It seemed really unfair that some people got parents who accepted everything they did. I thought about Kate, and how her mother and father never yelled and how they let her do what she wanted. How her mother and father liked the records she played. My parents hated Stevie's music; whenever Caribou practiced in the garage, Mom and Dad would go out to the shopping mall. But I loved listening; I would sit in a corner of the garage and love the way I could feel the bass thumping through the floor.

Now Stevie was leaving, and Dad didn't even seem

upset about it. And Mom just went along with whatever Dad thought. I wondered how they could be like that. Didn't they know how serious this was? Was I the only one who was so upset about it?

The Greyhound bus station was pretty empty this early in the morning. There were two old people sitting on either side of a huge box tied up with rope. There were two teenage girls sitting and giggling. The man behind the ticket counter looked very sleepy. Stevie went up to the window and bought his ticket. In my head I imagined that two policemen would come rushing out and arrest Stevie before he got on the bus. But nothing happened, of course. The ticket man barely looked up when Stevie said, "One way to Montreal."

We all sat down on the orange chairs and waited. None of us said anything. I looked around at the vending machines—soda and candy bars, and then one that sold little gifts. You could put a quarter in and get a plastic rain bonnet.

Finally the bus pulled up out front. An announcement came over the loudspeaker: "The bus to Montreal is now boarding."

Stevie jumped to his feet. "I've got to get this stuff on board," he said, and he began to slide his steamer trunk out the door. I could still see the Skylark decal on the side.

"Can we help?" Mom asked, but he waved her away.

There was a little commotion in the bus station, and the passengers lined up outside on the curb. The driver put the luggage in the luggage compartment and then collected the tickets. Stevie waited until the last minute. He stood with us, hopping from foot to foot in the cold. I knotted my woolen scarf tighter around my throat.

"Stevie, I want you to call home right away," Mom said. "Call collect. As soon as you settle in. I want to know what's going on."

"I will," Stevie said. "I promise."

"Here," Mom said, and she reached into her purse. She rummaged around in the big, lumpy bag for a while until she found her wallet. "I want you to take some money," she said. "A little extra."

"No, no," Stevie said. "I have enough, Mom."

Mom looked sadder than ever. She held a few bills crunched in her hand, and she didn't know what to do with them. For a second I thought she was just going to let them go—watch them fly away in the wind. She sighed and put them back into her wallet.

"I've got to go," Stevie said. "They're about to leave." He reached out and pulled my mother against him. He hugged her very tightly, and he buried his head in her coat. She kept patting his back, and I thought of her as a young mother then, burping her baby. She probably held Stevie like that when he was first born. She probably never let him out of her sight. Now she was saying goodbye to him for a very long time.

Finally Stevie pulled away from Mom. Then he came over to me and pulled me into him in the same way. I felt like he was about to swing me around in a square dance, like the ones we had in gym class. It was only all girls, though, but Jennifer Levitan was so strong that when you had her for a partner, she practically do-si-doed you into the wall.

Stevie hugged me very hard, and I could feel his jacket against my cheek. It was kind of rough but felt good. I barely came up to his shoulder, and he had to stoop down. He pulled away from me very soon; then he reached out and messed up my hair.

I saw that Stevie was starting to grow a mustache and beard; I hadn't even noticed it before. There was a little bit of darkness around his lip and on his chin.

Once I had stood in the bathroom and watched him shave. He had done it very carefully. The Jefferson Airplane was blasting on the stereo, and Stevie stood at the sink with his head lifted, pushing a razor along under his chin, which was covered with shaving cream. It was like he was digging a path through snow.

Maybe when I saw him next, he would look completely different. Maybe he would have a full beard and mustache. Maybe he would have gray hair. Or maybe, I thought, as Stevie climbed onto the bus, I never *would* see him again. He would forget about me. He would start a whole new life in Canada.

The folding doors groaned to a close, and the bus made a big sighing sound. Stevie walked down the aisle and took a seat by the window. He looked out through the dark blue glass. The bus began to pull away, but Stevie kept on looking.

PART TWO

CHAPTER 6

"Now we can finally do something with the garage," Dad said one morning at breakfast.

"Like what?" asked Mom.

"Store the lawn furniture inside instead of letting it get all rusty out back. Maybe buy some new power tools."

I sat and looked at him. It was just a few weeks after Stevie had left. The garage, which had been Stevie's rehearsal space, was still empty, the walls covered with the padding he and Gary and Peter had put up. I went alone into the garage and sang a few lines of a song out loud. I never sing when anyone is in the room because I don't have a good voice. In music class at school I was always a Listener.

But now Dad wanted to lug in the deck chairs from the yard and buy big drills and saws. He wanted to turn the garage into a workroom. "Finally I have my garage back," he said, as though it were really an even trade: a cold, damp room in exchange for Stevie.

I sat and looked away from him, looked out the window. Finally my father stood up. "I've got to be off," he said.

"Becca, you'd better get a move on, too," said Mom. "Kate will be waiting."

So I put my homework into my schoolbag and made sure that my barrettes were even. You get used to things—it's funny. I never thought I would be able to stand having Stevie so far away. I thought I would cry myself to sleep every night for the rest of my life. In the beginning I did, and then I would have terrible nightmares. I never remembered what they were about when I woke up. Then after a while the nightmares stopped, and I began to dream about normal, boring things. But still I thought a lot about Stevie. Every day I would be eating my lunch in the cafeteria, and all of a sudden I would remember that he was gone and that he wouldn't be there when I got home from school. That I would be all alone with my parents, and I had nothing to say to them. Kate always knew what I was thinking about. She could tell from my face. "It's your family, right?" she would ask, and I would nod.

But still life went on. My mother played cards with Mrs. Klein, Mrs. Bauer, and Mrs. Herzog, and my father watched television. I worked on my homework for Miss Brodskey's class and went to the skating rink with Kate after school. I liked going very fast around the edge, my blades slashing across the ice. I liked going so fast that all the other skaters became one big blur.

I wondered what Stevie was doing. I would be sitting there in the classroom, doing long division, and I would think: Somewhere in Canada my brother is doing something else. Maybe he's eating lunch. Or going to the bathroom. Or writing a letter. I hoped he was doing that most of all.

The first letter from Stevie came a week and a half after he left. It was addressed just to me. My mom got one from him the next day. She didn't make me read mine to her, and I was glad. This was private. He had already telephoned, so Mom knew that everything was okay. Calls from Canada are expensive, so we had only talked for three minutes. His voice sounded very different over the long-distance wire. The connection was bad, and everything he said made an echo.

"Hello, hello, Becca, Becca," came his voice. He told us that he was staying in a run-down house right in the middle of Montreal. The next day he would begin looking for a job. He didn't say much else.

And then the letter came. I got home from school and let myself in with my key. Mom was in the dining room playing cards. I could hear women's voices laughing and could smell cigarette smoke, which I hate. I went into the kitchen and poured myself a glass of milk. Mom had put a package of Twinkies out on the table, and I sat down and began to eat. That was when I noticed the letter. It was propped up against the bowl of fruit in the middle of the table. "Becca Silverman," it said. "15 Marsha Lane." It was really for me!

You have to understand that I never got much mail. Once when I was ten, I sent away to the Famous Artists School. I drew the picture of the lumberjack, like you were supposed to, and sent it in. Where you had to write your age, I said that I was forty. I made sure to write in script, so they would believe me. I sent it in and forgot about it.

One day a big package came in the mail. It was addressed to me. Inside there were other pictures that I was supposed to copy—one of a horse and another of a lady lying on a couch. But then I saw that you were supposed to send a lot of money in if you wanted them to look at your work. I would never have that much money, so I just threw the whole thing out. Then one day the doorbell rang, and I answered it. A man stood there in a suit and tie, carrying a briefcase.

"Hello there, little girl," he said. "Is your mother home?"

"Mom!" I called. "There's a man here!"

Mom came to the door in her bathrobe. "Yes?" she said. "Can I help you?"

"Mrs. Silverman, I'm from the Famous Artists School," the man said. "We were wondering why you have not sent your first assignment in. We wondered if perhaps you desired some home art lessons. I am a certified instructor of both figure and landscape drawing. I studied art at the Sorbonne in Paris, France."

My mother looked confused. "I never sent away for anything," she said.

"Aren't you Mrs. Becca Silverman?" the man asked.

"*No,*" said my mother, and then she turned to me. I stood a few inches behind her in the hallway. "Becca," she said, "did you send away for art lessons by any chance?"

I nodded; I couldn't speak. The man and my mother both stared at me. "There's been a mistake," my mother said. "I'm terribly sorry, sir. She's just a little girl, much too young for art lessons."

So the man went back down the walk, and Mom closed the door. I thought she was going to yell, but she didn't. All she said was "Please don't mention this to your father. And the next time you think about sending away for anything, please consult me or your father first."

That was the last interesting mail I got. Then came the letter from Stevie. I put down my Twinkie and held the letter up to the light. I could see his big handwriting inside. I ripped open the envelope.

Dear Becca,

     Here I am in Canada. Yes, I am completely fine, and the house is okay. I have a bedroom that gets a lot of sun. There are no curtains yet, so the light wakes me up every morning. I'm living with three other guys for a while, and we'll see how it works out. Their names are Daniel, Matthew, and Michel. The first two are from the U.S., and Michel is from Canada. They've been here for a few months, and Michel says he can definitely get me a job washing dishes at his friend's restaurant. Hey, Becca, I'm learning how to cook. Everybody chips in and helps make dinner. Last night I made beef stew. Mom would have been impressed.

It's really strange not knowing anybody here. I keep looking around for faces I know, but I don't find any. The city is pretty nice. Many people speak French, which I don't understand, of course, since I took woodworking in junior high instead of a language. Oh, well. You should learn French next year when they give you a choice. I bet you'd be good at it. Maybe you could teach me.

I hope you are doing okay at home. Take care of Skipper—slip him scraps under the table if you can.

> Love,
> Your brother, Stevie

The sounds from the bridge game seemed to disappear. I could only hear Stevie's voice in my head. I got my notebook out of my schoolbag and opened it to a clean page. I would write back right away. Stevie would get a letter from me and be so excited. He would read it to the other guys he lived with, and they all would wish that they had little sisters like me.

Dear Stevie,

I am sitting here eating my afternoon snack
and writing you a letter. I just got yours and was
very happy. It sounds scary to be in that new place.
I wish you were closer. I remember when we were
at Camp Skylark and you were all the way across
the woods and I couldn't talk to you when I wanted
to. It's like that now, but much worse. Mom and
Dad are being okay. But I can't talk to Dad because
I'm mad at him for being the way he is. So I just do
my dumb homework and see Kate after school.

Mr. and Mrs. Ruskin are really great. Sometimes I
think it's unfair that we didn't get them for parents.
Life would be very different if we had been in the
Ruskin family. I think they are perfect parents. They
let Kate do whatever she wants. She can come to
dinner anytime—she doesn't even have to call them.
They always just assume that she's with me. Also,
they never check to see that her homework is done.
They don't stand there reading her essays out loud,
like Mom and Dad do. And here's the weirdest part
of all! Last week her parents had a dinner party and
Kate and I were playing in her room. We went into
the kitchen to find the scissors for Kate's scrapbook
when we smelled something funny. Then I suddenly
knew what it was. Remember I told you about how
the police chief came to Mrs. Lazenby's class last
year and talked about drugs? He lit this pellet and
said, "This is what marijuana smells like, boys and
girls. Like burning rope." Mr. and Mrs. Ruskin were
smoking marijuana with their friends! I told Kate,

and she said, "Oh, I know that. They smoke it once in a while." I couldn't believe it. Imagine if Mom and Dad knew. There was a lot of laughing going on in that living room. It sounded better than Mom's bridge games. I wish I had been born a Ruskin. Then Kate and I would be sisters. You could be our brother, too. Oh, well, I can't think of anything more to say right now. I will write you letters all the time. I'm going to save up my money to come visit you someday soon. Do they have good shows on TV there?

    Love,
    Becca

Mom came into the room just as I was finishing the letter. "I didn't hear you come home, dear," she said. "I would have said hello sooner. Do you want to pop your head in and say hello to the ladies?"

"Okay," I said. "Let me finish this first." I ate the rest of the Twinkie, then found an envelope and stamp in the mail drawer. I addressed the letter and put it in the mail basket next to the refrigerator. Then I went with Mom into the dining room. The air was filled with smoke. Not marijuana smoke, of course.

"Look who I found," Mom said, standing behind me. She put her hands on my shoulders.

Everyone made little clucking noises. "She's looking *beautiful,* Harriet," one of the ladies said.

"What grade are you in now?" Mrs. Herzog asked me.

"Sixth," I said.

"I hope you don't have that awful Miss Brodskey," she said with a laugh. "My Alex had her a few years ago, and it was *not* a pleasant year for him."

"I do have her," I said. "But she's okay."

"Whoops, I'm sorry," Mrs. Herzog said.

Everybody laughed. The air was so smoky that I began to cough. "Can I go upstairs now?" I asked Mom.

She nodded. "Bye," I said to the ladies, and they all said goodbye together, like it had been rehearsed. As I went up the steps, I could hear them murmuring things about me. ". . . and even starting to get a real bustline, Harriet," someone said.

I went into my room and stood in front of my mirror. Was it true? I hadn't really begun to develop yet, not like my friend Emma, who had gotten her period at ten and already looked like she was in college or something. But me, I just looked twelve. There was a little something under my blouse—not enough to wear a bra yet. Maybe next year. I wasn't in a big hurry anyway. Sometimes when we got changed for gym class, I could see how Emma's bra straps dug into her shoulders, leaving little red marks. It didn't look very comfortable. Kate's mother never wore a bra, Kate said. There's no law that says you have to wear one, Mrs. Ruskin told her. My mom wore a bra *and* a girdle. When she got dressed to go out for the evening, sometimes I stood and watched.

She sucked in her stomach really hard and then yanked her girdle up. "Uch!" she said. "That's tight!" But still she wore it.

I wondered if I would be like Mom when I grew up.

71

I knew I'd have to change a lot for that to happen. I'd practically have to stop talking. The only person I really had anything in common with was Kate, and we weren't even related. Stevie and me, it's not that we had a lot in common. It's just that we happened to have the same family to talk about. And we could mention all the vacations we went on a long time ago. "Remember Hershey, Pennsylvania?" I asked him once.

It was a town where they made Hershey's chocolate. We walked through the factory and saw where they cooked everything. Little drops of chocolate came out of a machine and were molded into chocolate bars. Then they went up on a long conveyor belt, where they got wrapped in paper. At the end of the tour everyone got free chocolate Kisses to take home. Stevie and I sat in the back of the station wagon on the way to the motel, eating until we both felt like throwing up. But neither of us really did throw up.

Then there was the trip to Old Sturbridge Village. This was a place where you saw what life was like in colonial times. You walked into cottages where people were dressed up in old-fashioned costumes. A lady sat in front of a big vat of wax, dipping a long piece of string until it turned into a candle. I thought it might be nice to stay in that cottage forever. It would be like living inside a history book. People would come and go, but as long as they stayed in that room, they would never grow up or anything. They would stay in the past forever. Of course, I knew this wasn't really true, but I pretended that it was. I watched the lady as she dipped candles—lowering her arm and then raising it again. She looked very happy. Maybe she really did think it was the 1600's.

Stevie had been with me on these trips. That was what was so great about having a brother—he knew about certain things without having to be told. He just understood. When Mom and Dad used to fight, Stevie would come into my room, or I'd go into his room, and we'd clap our hands over our ears and hum.

"Oh, Stevie," I said out loud. "What are you doing now?" Maybe he was standing in front of his own mirror in Montreal, looking at himself, too. There was no way to know. I wanted to go visit him very much. If I started saving up my money, then maybe I could afford to go to Canada. It would take a lot of baby-sitting jobs to do that.

I actually liked baby-sitting. It all depended on who you were sitting for and what kind of food they had in their house. I had only baby-sat three times in my life so far.

The Reynolds family around the corner on Joanne Street had a color TV and huge bags of Snickers bars, and their kid was four years old and very silly. I had a good time when I baby-sat for him. So I decided that making money would be my big goal for the year. I would get as many baby-sitting jobs as I could. I would make enough money to take a bus to Canada.

That night Kate asked me to go to the movies, and I almost said yes, but then changed my mind. I would have to start saving every penny now if I wanted to see Stevie again.

CHAPTER 7

With everything that had been going on in the house, I had forgotten about something big. Every year in school there was an art contest. And every year I lost.

"Oh, you'll definitely win this time," Janette always said, but I never did. There was a wall in the auditorium that had a new mural painted on it every spring by the winner of the contest. The winner also got a check for $100.

The contest had a different theme each year. The year before, it was "The World of Sports," which, as you can probably guess, I didn't find too exciting. A boy won, and he painted a football field on the wall and a lot of people sitting in the bleachers, yelling. He put balloons over the people's heads, with the words "Yay!" or "Go, team!"

This year, if I were picked, I could use the money to go visit Stevie in Canada. It was a great idea.

Now Miss Brodskey stood in front of the class, reading us the rules of the contest, even though we heard them every year.

When she was done, everybody began to whisper. Kate was about to lean over and say something to me, but Miss Brodskey started to talk again. "The theme of this year's contest is 'My Country, 'Tis of Thee,' " she said. "The winner will be expected to create a patriotic mural, to celebrate our nation." Kate turned to me and rolled her eyes.

I could hardly wait until lunch hour, when I could talk about it with my friends. But first we had to do long division, and I made so many mistakes that my pencil eraser wore down to nothing. Finally lunchtime came. I stood on the cafeteria line, sliding my tray along the metal slats.

" 'My Country, 'Tis of Thee!' " said Kate. "Who feels patriotic these days?"

"Not me," I mumbled, and it was true. A patriotic mural was about the last thing in the world I felt like painting. But still, I thought, if I won the contest, I would get to go to Canada, and that was what I cared about most of all. I could pretend to feel patriotic; no one would have to know how I really felt.

"I know you'll win," said Janette, like always.

"Yeah, right," I said. "Fat chance."

All during lunch I kept thinking about being given $100 and taking a bus to Montreal. I just had to win.

I talked to Mom and Dad about the contest at dinner. "I've just got to win this year," I said, but I didn't tell them why.

"Hold your horses, Becca," Dad said. "You never know what could happen. Somebody else could prove to be the new Picasso—somebody in another class."

"Everyone says that I'm the best artist," I said. I heard my voice and realized how I sounded, but I didn't care. I had no idea whether or not my parents would actually let me go visit Stevie. But it was a long time off; I didn't have to think about it yet. I would cross that bridge when I came to it, as my dad always said.

I stayed up late all week, drawing in my sketch pad. I drew pictures of horses, and ballerinas, and then a picture of the seashore. On Friday the principal was coming to our art class, and I wanted to make sure that I was in top shape. He was going to walk around and look at everybody's work and pick five finalists out of the whole school. Then those five kids would have to submit a sketch and write a page about what they wanted to paint for the contest, and the best idea would win.

I wore a clean smock over my blouse on Friday. We were painting self-portraits. Mr. Cable, the principal, must have been sick of looking at art; he had been to visit the art classes all week. Most kids were painting normal pictures of themselves just standing there, facing forward. Maureen Startz was such a bad artist that she just painted a stick figure with big black eyes and a crooked smile.

I decided to draw myself in a mirror. I painted a frame around the edge of the painting, and I made the whole thing kind of silvery. At the bottom I painted a small photograph of Stevie, like it was stuck in the frame of the mirror. Behind me I painted my bedroom. You could just see the edge of my bed and my night table. It was one of the best things I had done all year in art class.

Mr. Cable knocked on the door of the classroom. The art teacher, Mrs. Green, said, "Come in!" in a very cheerful voice.

Mr. Cable was tall and thin, and his suit hung on him like he was a clothes hanger. "Good morning, boys and girls," he said. He wrung his hands together as he talked. He said "ahem" a lot, too. "I guess, ahem, you know why I'm, ahem, here," he said. "I would like to look at all of your artwork, so that I can decide on the five finalists for the contest." He said it as though he were apologizing. I wondered how he had gotten to be principal.

He walked around the class with a notebook in his hand. He asked you your name and wrote it down. Then he looked at your work and made funny marks in his book. I watched as he looked at Maureen Startz's painting. He stood squinting at it, pretending to take it very seriously. I knew he was just being nice. Finally he came up behind me.

"I'm Becca Silverman," I said, even though he already knew. Mr. Cable just stood there, watching me paint. I faked it since there wasn't really too much left to do. I just pretended to be touching up the hair with yellow.

"Well, well," Mr. Cable said. "This is very interesting!" I was the only one he had said something to. Everyone looked at me enviously. He stood there for a few more seconds, tilting his head to the side, and then he moved on, to where Kate was trying hard to get her self-portrait to look like herself. It looked like a cartoon character, no matter how much she tried to make it real. A few easels down, Tommy Vesco was painting a picture of himself with a Superman cape on, blowing in the wind. The principal and Tommy were very familiar with each other because Tommy was always being sent down to his office.

"Thank you, class," Mr. Cable finally said when he had looked at everybody's work. "I have been to all the classrooms now, and Monday I will announce the five finalists over the loudspeaker after the Pledge of Allegiance."

I went home with Kate after school that day. Snow was blowing around in the streets. At the Ruskins' Kate's mother was busy typing. I could hear the fast clatter of keys and the occasional bing when she came to the end of the line. Kate's father was home, too. He was sitting in the den with his feet up, grading papers. It was always weird to see somebody's father home in the middle of the afternoon.

Kate and I went to her refrigerator to get an afternoon snack, but there was nothing good. Just weird stuff in plastic containers: eggplant salad, some kind of seeds, and something that looked like a white sponge floating in water. We ended up scraping a couple of carrots and bringing them upstairs.

We sat down on her bed, which was just a mattress on the floor. I had begged my mother to let me do the same with my bed, but she said, "Absolutely not. We paid your uncle Leonard a lot of money to buy you that bed. Isn't it enough that we let you paint your walls?"

Kate had a huge poster of the Beatles on her wall. It was a very early photograph, and they had those bowl haircuts and were wearing suits. They looked very young. Like Stevie and Gary and Peter, I thought. On the opposite wall there was another poster of the Beatles, but this time they were older, wearing flowered jackets and with lots of hair. John Lennon had those wonderful round eyeglasses, and he looked very wise. He was holding up his hand in a peace sign. He didn't look anything like Stevie here, but still I was reminded of my brother. I held my own hand up in a peace sign and placed it against the smooth surface of the poster. Now my hand and John Lennon's were touching. This was probably as close as we would ever get.

It occurred to me then that this sort of thing would happen a lot in life: I would desperately want something and never get it. I just wanted to *meet* John Lennon, sit and talk with him for a little while—not jump all over him like a teenybopper and cut off a lock of his hair. I just wanted to have a conversation with him.

I had written him a letter but never mailed it. I knew that he would never have read it anyway. Once when I went over to Emma's house, she had a huge stack of old *Tiger Beat* magazines, and we sat all afternoon and looked through them. There was a contest where you got to spend a day with your favorite Beatle.

"Tell us, in 100 words or less, why you think you ought to win this chance of a lifetime," it read. And then in a later issue, somewhere lower down in the stack, I found the page where they told you who had won and showed photographs of the big day.

The winner was a girl from Tennessee named Candy Norton. She was holding her arms around Ringo Starr's chest. She had written her contest entry in the form of a poem: "You make me want to dance-oh/You make me want to sing-oh/You make me want to spend a/lifetime with you, Ringo."

There was a picture of her and Ringo having dinner in an Italian restaurant. He was feeding her spaghetti from a fork. Then there they were swimming together in a pool. It was probably the best day of her life. But Ringo Starr was probably laughing at her inside, and she would never know it. If I ever met John Lennon, I didn't want it to be that way.

But the chances of my really meeting him didn't seem too great. I lived with my mother and father on Marsha Lane, and nothing big ever happened there. All I was supposed to do was keep doing my homework every day.

It wasn't enough anymore. I thought about Stevie, way up there in Canada. He had made his statement. He had told me to find my own way of making a statement. Be original, he had said.

"Oh, I really hope you win," said Kate. I had told her why I wanted to win so badly this year. I always told Kate everything, of course.

"Thanks, I hope so, too," I said. "I can't stop thinking about it."

"I wish I could paint like you," said Kate, and then she crunched down on a carrot stick.

"Well, I wish I could do math like you," I said.

"It's not the same," said Kate. "You know it's not. Math is a skill; art is a talent. My mom said that. I may be smart, but I'll never be a genius. Leonardo da Vinci was a genius."

"So was Albert Einstein," I said.

We just sat and looked at each other. "Look," I said, "I know something you have that I don't have. Something I would give anything for."

"What?" she asked.

"Your parents," I said quietly, and I knew it was true. I *would* have traded in my parents for the Ruskins. It was probably a terrible thing to say, but I felt it. Imagine having Kate's mom and dad for parents. At the dinner table everybody was friendly and made jokes. Once there was even a little food fight at Kate's house. Her father flung a couple of peas at her mother. "You're a silly man, Max," she said to him, but she bonked him over the head with a breadstick anyway.

The Ruskins went interesting places on weekends, too. One time Kate asked if she could take me along, and her parents said "of course." We went far out into the country, to an old farmhouse. There were a lot of cars parked in the field. A big party was going on in the house, with lots of pies and eggnog and singing. Kids ran around among the adults; nobody cared or made them stay in the playroom. Three little girls in long white dresses, wreaths in their hair, shrieked and chased each other through the house.

There was a boy about our age there, and he was very skinny, with braces and bell-bottoms. "Hi, girls," he said. "Want to see my pet?"

We said okay, and he led me and Kate into his bedroom. There was a glass tank on the windowsill, and it had a snake in it. He cradled the snake in his arms like it was a kitten. "Uch, that's disgusting!" said Kate.

"His name is Orville," the boy said. "He doesn't bite. Want to hold him?"

"Never!" Kate said, but I looked at the snake and suddenly it didn't seem so scary.

"I'll hold him," I said.

Orville wound around my wrist like a bracelet and then climbed up onto my shoulder. He coiled around my neck, but it didn't hurt. His skin was shiny, but not wet at all.

We finally left the house in the early evening. I had never eaten that much pie in my entire life. We were still singing rounds in the car on the way home. The

Ruskins had actually gotten me to sing in front of them.

"Who lives in that house?" I asked. "Who are that kid's parents?"

"Oh, it's a communal household," Mrs. Ruskin said. "Several families live there, and they all take part in the work and the child raising."

When Kate spent the day with me and my parents, we usually did something like go to the shopping mall. Once we drove out to Uncle Leonard's furniture store. I was worried that Kate would be bored, but she kept insisting that it was very interesting. Uncle Leonard had just gotten water beds in stock, and he let us try them out.

"Here, you two, sit right down," my uncle said.

I sat hesitantly on the edge. I thought the bed would burst, like a balloon. "Don't be afraid," he said, and then I rested my full weight on the bed. Inside, water sloshed around like a bath. I could feel it moving. The bed was warm; it felt like it was alive and breathing. I put my feet up and closed my eyes. Underneath me, the whole bed seemed to sway. It was like I was doing the back-float at the town pool. Mom and Dad and Uncle Leonard went off elsewhere in the store, leaving me and Kate alone. She got on the other side of the bed.

"I'm seasick," she said after a minute, and we both laughed.

We got off the bed and walked around the store. There were couches that looked like giant marshmallows, and couches covered in crackling plastic. At Janette's house her parents put plastic on all the furniture and gates up in the living room so children couldn't come in.

Kate and I tried out a couple of Uncle Leonard's reclining chairs. Uncle Leonard is my dad's brother. He is only a year older than Dad, and very quiet. He is married to my aunt Pearl, and they don't have any kids. They keep to themselves, my father says.

On the day I took Kate to the store, my uncle said, "So, what do you hear from that son of yours, Herb?"

My father shook his head. "Nothing much," he said. "He's living his life. What can I do about it, Len?"

My uncle shook his head. "Herb, if he were *my* son," he said, "well, I wouldn't let him chicken out like that. It's the principle of the thing."

"Easy for you to say," Dad said. "You can't tell nineteen-year-olds what to do."

"But you *can* tell them that you won't have anything more to do with them," Uncle Leonard said.

We were all sitting down now on a sofa and fancy chairs, like it was somebody's real home. The only difference was that all the furniture had price tags on it. Kate and I sat next to each other on a shaggy gray couch. We didn't say anything. Dad and Uncle Leonard were facing each other in big armchairs. Mom was sitting on a footstool. There was a coffee table in the middle of the fake room and even books on the bookshelves. A lamp was on, throwing a pale light on the scene.

"I've pretty much washed my hands of the matter, Len," Dad said. "I haven't given him any encouragement. And not a single penny either."

"Well, that makes sense," said Uncle Leonard. "Did you watch Nixon on the tube last night? The guy knows what he's doing."

My dad nodded. "He's okay," he said.

"Look," my uncle said, "you people have to come out to the house soon. Pearl's doing a lot with the place."

"Sure, sure," Dad said. He stood up to leave. We all followed. At the glass doors of the store Dad and Uncle Leonard leaned forward like they were going to hug, but all they did was thump each other on the back. When Uncle Leonard reached out to kiss me, like he always did, I turned my face.

In the car on the way home I whispered to Kate, "I'm sorry that wasn't much fun."

"It was very interesting," she said. "I swear."

But it wasn't anything like that day we spent with her parents. There was no dancing, no running around, and no good food. And during the drive back to our town my father didn't suddenly burst into a rendition of "Michael, Row the Boat Ashore," like Mr. Ruskin had. It had started to rain now. The only sound in the car came from the windshield wipers, slowly whining as they moved back and forth across the glass.

CHAPTER 8

ON MONDAY MORNING, RIGHT AFTER THE PLEDGE OF Allegiance, Mr. Cable's voice came over the loudspeaker in the classroom. "Good morning, boys and girls," he said.

"Good morning," we all said back, even though he couldn't possibly hear us.

"As you remember from last week, today is the day I am going to announce the finalists in the schoolwide art contest. I'd like to say, first of all, that everybody's work was very impressive. You are all growing up to be budding artists. I wouldn't be surprised if we have a Rembrandt or two among you." Mr. Cable chuckled.

Kate and I looked at each other and rolled our eyes. "I have a list here of the five students whose work impressed me the most," the principal said. "Each of these students will submit a sketch and a page of writing to me, explaining what he would paint on the mural if he were to win. On Friday, at the big assembly, I shall announce the grand prizewinner. Remember, the theme of this contest is 'My Country, 'Tis of Thee.' The prize, which will be delivered when the mural is finished, is a check for one hundred dollars."

Kate leaned over and whispered to me, "If he ever loses his job, he'd make a great game show host!"

There was a rustling over the loudspeaker. Mr. Cable found the piece of paper with the finalists' names on it. Please, I thought. Let it be me. Please let it be me.

"Eleanor Truitt," said Mr. Cable. "The first finalist is Eleanor Truitt."

A couple of kids groaned. Eleanor was in the other sixth-grade class. She got perfect grades.

"Tommy Vesco," said Mr. Cable.

A gasp rose up in the class. Nobody could believe it! Tommy held his arms up over his head, like a prizefighter congratulating himself.

"Melissa Barry," Mr. Cable said.

She was in the fourth grade, and I didn't know her too well. There were only two names left now. I sat and listened, crossing my fingers. This was almost like the Vietnam lottery. Everything hinged on what we heard.

My brother's life had been changed that night. This wasn't so dramatic, but still it seemed pretty big to me. I wanted to paint the mural in the auditorium very much, but even more than that, I wanted to go spend the summer with Stevie.

"Danny Ellman," Mr. Cable said. Danny was a quiet kid in the fifth grade. I had seen his drawings before, and they were pretty good. There was only one name left. I just had to get picked!

My heart sank. I wasn't going to win. Somebody else's name was going to be called. After school I would come home and eat my snack and drink a glass of milk, and I would sit at the table feeling sorry for myself. Maybe Kate would be there and we would go listen to the Beatles for a while, but it wouldn't help. And at dinnertime my father would say, "See, Becca? Now maybe you'll be a little more realistic about things in the future."

He would be right, too. I shouldn't have built my hopes up. I slumped down in my seat, and Mr. Cable's voice came through the speaker loud and clear. "Rebecca Silverman," he said.

The name echoed in my head for a moment. It was really me! I had been picked! Kate reached out and squeezed my hand. All the heads in the class swiveled in my direction. Tommy Vesco and I looked at each other. We finally had something in common.

As I walked home from school that day, snowflakes landed softly in my hair. Kate held out her hands, palms up. "This may be one of the last snowfalls this winter," she said.

I knew she was disappointed that she hadn't been one of the finalists. She kept saying that she didn't have a chance, but still she must have felt bad. I wanted to cheer her up. Inside me, though, all I could think about was painting the mural. I saw myself standing on a tall ladder with a paintbrush in my hand. All alone in the huge room. And then I saw myself cashing in the check for $100 and buying a round-trip ticket to Montreal. I saw Stevie standing at the gate of the bus station in Canada, holding out his arms to me.

"Do you want to come over?" I asked Kate.

"Nah," she said. "I have a headache. I want to get started on the math homework anyway."

We said goodbye at the corner, and I watched her walk off. "Kate!" I called out.

She turned around and stood there shivering. "What?" she asked.

I didn't really have anything to say to her; I don't know why I called out her name. "Nothing," I said. "I'll see you tomorrow."

That night at dinner I still had to listen to my father tell me about holding my horses. But I could tell that he was proud of me anyway. He held up his water glass and made a toast: "To my daughter, the artist, who certainly didn't get her talent from me!"

I felt good for a few minutes, but then it died down. I realized that Mom and Dad were probably comparing me to Stevie. They thought I was the good kid, the one to be proud of.

I was about to start my dessert. Mom had baked an

apple cobbler, which I always loved. "Stevie's done a lot of good things, too," I said.

Mom and Dad looked at me. "We haven't said anything about him, dear," Mom said.

"Well, I know what you're thinking," I said. "How I'm a success and he's a disappointment. I heard Dad and Uncle Leonard talking at the store."

Dad put down his glass. "Sometimes, Becca," he said, "you talk about things that you don't really understand. You can't possibly know what you're talking about; you're too young. There is a very serious war going on in Vietnam. It's not some big board game. I fought in a war; I know what it's all about. I helped defeat Hitler's men, and I felt very proud of myself for it. Stevie was asked to help serve his country as an able-bodied soldier. He chose to shirk that responsibility. I can't pretend to feel pride for him when I don't really feel it."

"He could have gotten killed," I said, and all of a sudden I was shouting. "Did you want him to get killed?" I asked. "He's my brother!"

My mother looked around. "Oh, how did everything get like this?" she asked. "Things used to be so much easier." She looked like she was going to cry. I didn't want to watch.

"Can I be excused?" I asked. Dad nodded, and I took my dessert upstairs. I lay down on my bed and looked at the paintings on the walls for a while. It made me feel like I was somewhere far away from everything.

Then I did something that I had never done before. I

got down on my knees next to the bed, and I prayed. My family is Jewish, but we never paid too much attention to religion, except on Yom Kippur, when we didn't eat all day.

I guess sometimes I believed in God. Usually when I was alone, walking through the woods near the school. Things just seemed so peaceful and pretty then that I thought there just had to be a God. But then other times I didn't believe in anything at all. The only person I ever talked about this with was Kate. She didn't believe in God, and neither did her parents. My mom and dad always said that they believed in God, but that you don't have to go to a temple to pray. You could do it right in the house, Mom said.

So I knelt there on the floor, and I formed my hands into a steeple, like you're supposed to. "Please," I said, "let me win the contest in school. I want to win it more than anything, and not just so I will be more popular in school and have everyone think I'm talented but also because I want to use the money to go visit Stevie in Canada. I miss him very much." I paused. Was there something I had left out? I couldn't think of anything. "Thank you," I said at the end, as though I had been talking to an operator on the telephone.

The next day Kate stayed home from school. I waited on our corner, but she just didn't show up, so I went on alone. In the schoolyard a couple of people came up and congratulated me. "I just knew you'd get it," said Susan Levitt.

And in class Miss Brodskey announced that she was very proud of both me and Tommy. "Imagine," she said. "Two finalists in this very class. What a talented bunch of students you all are."

I felt flushed with happiness, but the day just didn't seem the same without Kate there. During lunch hour I called her house on the pay phone. Mrs. Ruskin answered. "Hi," I said. "This is Becca. I'm calling for Kate. Is she okay?"

"Oh, she just has a little cold, Becca," Mrs. Ruskin said. "She's taking a nap now. Maybe you'd like to stop by on your way home from school. I know that would cheer her up."

I said I would, and then I went back into the cafeteria. "Here, I'll split my brownie with you," Janette offered, but I wasn't really hungry. I started doodling on a napkin, planning what I would draw for the contest. Mr. Cable was going to pick one of us Friday on the basis of our ideas and sketches for the mural. Tonight I would have to come up with an idea.

The bell rang, and everyone filed back into their classrooms. The cafeteria lady was left to deal with the mess on all the tables. In class I sat at my desk for the rest of the day, watching the light snow blow around outside. I kept looking over to whisper something to Kate, but her seat was still empty.

At the end of the day I stopped off at the Ruskins' house and brought Kate the homework assignment. She was sitting up in bed, listening to the Beatles, of course.

"Hi," she said when I came in.

"How are you feeling?" I asked.

"Oh, okay," she said. "It's just a dumb cold." She reached out and shut off the stereo. Her nose was red, and her bed was littered with crumpled-up tissues.

"Are you mad at me?" I blurted out. "Did I do something?"

Kate looked down. "I just got depressed in school yesterday," she said. "I don't know if I'll ever win anything in my life. All you kept talking about was wanting to win the contest, and I knew I had no chance, but it was like I hadn't even entered at all. Like I didn't count."

"I'm sorry, Kate," I said. I felt terrible.

"Well, forget about it," Kate said. "Do you want to play Scrabble with me? I've been trying to get my parents to play all day, but they said they were busy."

"Sure," I said, and I went and got the maroon box from her game chest. She had forgiven me; it was as easy as that. We played Scrabble for half an hour, and Kate won by almost 100 points.

"You didn't let me win because of what I said, did you?" she asked, and I had to swear to her that I didn't.

When I left, I felt a lot better about things between me and Kate. I hugged her, even though she was all germy. "I hope you're well enough to come to school tomorrow," I said. "I don't know how I'll survive."

"I'll be there," she said.

On my way out I passed the kitchen, where Mr. Ruskin was cooking. He was standing at the stove with an apron on over his pants. He was stirring a pot of something.

"Becca, taste this!" he called out to me, and I went into the kitchen. I was a little embarrassed, but I let him fill the big wooden spoon and give me a taste of the vegetable soup he was cooking.

"It's terrific," I said, and it really was. Mr. Ruskin was the only father I knew who actually did things like cooking and cleaning. When I went to Janette's house on weekends, her father was always lying underneath the car, fixing it. Janette and I would walk by and see his feet sticking out. My father was good at doing things like hanging paintings or hooking up electrical appliances. It was really nice to see Mr. Ruskin in the kitchen, having a good time. I just wanted to sit down at the table and never leave.

"How are things at home, Becca?" he asked.

"Oh, not so hot," I said.

"Because of Stevie?" he asked. He seemed to know everything.

"Yes," I said. "Dad only has bad things to say about him. It doesn't get any better."

Mr. Ruskin lowered the heat under his pot of soup, then put the lid back on. "That's rough," he said. "The only thing to do, Becca, is to keep on believing what you feel is right. Don't give up."

Mr. Ruskin looked at me with his small, bright eyes. His face was almost entirely hidden beneath his thick beard—he looked like Santa Claus as a young man. He looked like someone who would come into a room carrying gifts. If I had a father like Mr. Ruskin, I thought, then everything would be different.

It isn't fair, I kept thinking, but then I realized that a lot of things weren't fair. My brother was living somewhere far away in another country. That wasn't fair. There was a big war going on in the world, and people were getting killed every day. That wasn't fair either.

I went home, and dinner was already waiting on the table. "There you are," Mom said, looking at her watch. "I was getting worried. Herb!" she called. "Dinner!"

Dad came into the room, folding the newspaper in half. He took off his eyeglasses and cleaned them with his handkerchief. Then he put them back on. "I'm very hungry, Harriet," he said. "I hope you made something good."

"Stew," said Mom.

"Great," said Dad.

Mom served us, and I ate a big helping of the stew. It was one of her best dishes. "So," Dad said to me after a few minutes of silence, "tell us what you're planning on painting for that contest of yours. What idea have you come up with?"

I shrugged. "Nothing yet," I said. "I thought I'd try to figure something out after dinner tonight."

"That's a good idea," said Mom. "Make sure you do all your homework first, though."

"Okay," I said. I always did my homework, and Mom knew that. She just liked to say it. I think it made her feel like a mother on a TV show or something.

So after dinner and helping to clean up the kitchen, I went up to my room. Early evening was my favorite time of day there. I had a lamp on the desk that I turned on, and the room looked warm and interesting. I liked to sit at my desk then and write or draw.

I quickly did the homework—a few math problems that I wasn't sure I got right. I always went into a panic about math, and then Kate would sit down with me and slowly explain how an equation worked, and it would make perfect sense. But I needed her there to explain it to me.

I sat for a long time trying to come up with an idea for the mural. I looked around at my own walls, but they weren't much help. I couldn't draw animals in the auditorium; they didn't have anything to do with the topic. I would have to draw *people*. Doing what? I wondered. It had to be something patriotic.

Then all of a sudden it hit me. A parade! That was patriotic all right. I could draw a group of people marching in a parade, carrying flags.

I remembered the Memorial Day parade from a few years ago. Stevie was in the high school band, playing trumpet, and we all went to watch him march. It was one of the hottest days ever. I was eating a Good Humor bar, and the vanilla kept dripping down between my fingers. Dad kept pressing a handkerchief to his forehead. Mom stood and fanned herself with a magazine.

We lined up at the curb with everyone else and waited for the parade to begin. Finally we could hear music in the distance, and soon the marching band began making their way up the street. They were wearing red uniforms and leading the whole parade. I searched the faces until I found Stevie. His curly hair stuck out at the sides of his tall hat. His sheet music was clipped to the end of his trumpet, so he could read it as he marched.

I screamed and cheered and yelled Stevie's name out a few times. Stevie was marching right on the end, and he saw me just as he was about to go past. He winked right at me. That's my brother! I wanted to tell everyone, but then I realized that most of them probably had brothers or sisters or kids marching in the parade, too. And in a second the high school band had moved on down the street, and we were left with the next group: baton twirlers.

They wore silver sequined costumes and threw their batons way up into the air. One girl shrieked as her baton flew up over everyone's head and landed with a thump on the awning of a store.

There had been a lot of flags that day, I remembered. Little boys held huge American flags. There was no breeze, so the flags stood still. But if you were painting a mural, you would want to make the scene more interesting, so you would make the flags ripple in the wind.

I would draw a marching band, and at the front of it there would be two people, a boy and a girl, carrying flags. It was a great idea, I thought, and I quickly made a sketch and wrote down a paragraph about it to hand in the next morning.

I don't know how I got through the next few days, but somehow I did. Kate came back to school, and we passed notes to each other all day. "THIS IS SOOOOOOOOOOO BORING!!!!" she wrote during social studies.

On Friday at the big assembly Mr. Cable would announce the winner of the contest. Everyone in school was talking about it. The five finalists handed in our sketches and our paragraphs. I wondered what Tommy Vesco had written—probably something about having Uncle Sam wearing a cape and flying over the city like a super hero. Tommy's whole life seemed to center on comic books.

On Friday morning I slept right through my alarm, and Mom had to come in and wake me up. "Come on, sleepyhead," she said. "Today's the day."

I was very nervous. Kate and I walked to school together, not saying a word. She just seemed to know that I didn't want to talk. Right after the pledge everyone in the school went into the auditorium and waited for the assembly to begin. Mr. Cable walked onstage and went up to the microphone.

"Testing," he said, "one, two, three. Testing, one, two, three." The microphone began to shriek, and everyone covered their ears. Finally the shriek died down.

"Good morning, boys and girls," Mr. Cable said.

"Good morning," we all said at once, and then the assembly began.

CHAPTER 9

Mr. Cable made us wait. I couldn't believe it! He said that he would announce the winner of the contest at the *end* of the assembly. Everybody groaned.

Today we were being shown a movie. The movie monitor pulled the white screen down onstage, and someone shut off the overhead lights. The projector started up, and the sound track was in slow motion for a moment, like a record being played at the wrong speed. On the screen there was a swirl of colors, like Stevie's lava lamp, and then the words "DRUGS AND YOU."

First they showed a girl sitting in her bedroom, looking at a red pill in her hand. Then her voice came over the sound track, as though she were thinking out loud. "Should I . . . or shouldn't I?" she asked.

"Only *you* can make that choice," came a man's voice out of nowhere. "Let's see what might happen to Sally. . . ."

Then they cut to a scene with the same girl, later on, sitting in a corner of her bedroom with her hands in front of her face. The room started to spin around, and everything looked like it was being seen in a fun house mirror. She stood up and walked around the room as though she were in a fog. She held her hands out in front of her and began laughing for no reason. Then all of a sudden she started to cry. It was very creepy. They showed a close-up of her face, and she looked crazy.

In a second her mother came into the room. "Sally, Sally, what's wrong?" her mother asked. She began to shake the girl by her shoulders, but Sally just kept crying.

It was a very spooky movie. I wondered if LSD was really like this. I never wanted to try it. My bedroom looked weird enough as it was, with all that stuff painted on the walls. At the end of the movie the man's voice said, "Sally made a bad choice. But you—you can make a good choice. Don't do drugs."

The lights were turned back on, and we all squinted in the brightness for a moment. Mr. Cable came back onstage. "I hope that was informative," he said. "There will be more discussion groups about drugs in your classes next week."

He cleared his throat. "And now," he said, "it's time for what you've all been waiting for. I am now going to announce the winner of the mural contest. I have chosen this person on the basis of artistic talent and a good idea for the mural. The winner of the one hundred dollars is—" He paused dramatically, like he was saying who won Miss America. "The winner is . . . *Rebecca Silverman!*" he said right into the microphone. His voice was so loud that it seemed to thunder out. It was as though God were calling my name.

Everyone turned and looked at me. People began to whisper. A lot of people smiled and pointed. Then everyone applauded. The assembly finally ended, and we went back to class, but all the way down the hall, different people kept coming up to me and congratulating me. Kate stayed right by my side, smiling.

During reading hour Miss Brodskey came over to my desk to congratulate me. "You have brought a great honor to this class, Becca," she said. But later that day a rubber band went zinging against my arm. I looked up quickly and saw that Tommy Vesco had a satisfied smile on his face.

That night I wrote a long letter to Stevie. I told him all about winning the mural contest. I wrote the letter in three different colors of Magic Marker. I told him about my plan to come visit him in the summer, and I asked if it was okay with him. I wrote about everything that was on my mind: Mom and Dad, and Kate, and junior high school. I asked him if it was true that in junior high you can't go to the bathroom because the older kids try to make you smoke pot in there. I worked on the letter for an hour, and when I was done, I put Snoopy stickers all over the envelope, and then I mailed it.

In a week and a half there was an answer from Stevie. I came home from school with Kate, and there it was. She sat down across from me at the table and watched as I read the letter. "Do you want to hear it?" I asked, and she nodded. I figured that there probably wasn't too much Stevie would write that Kate couldn't hear. I told her everything, anyway.

Dear Becca,

I got your letter—thanks. I don't get too much mail up here in Canada. Nina said that she would write me a lot, but lately I haven't heard from her. I think she's forgetting about me. C'est la vie, as they say here. I haven't met anyone new in Canada. There are a couple of nice waitresses at the restaurant—hippie student types—but no one I'd like for a girl friend.

Congratulations about the contest; I told you what a terrific artist you are. Remember the time you painted the caribou antlers on the drum for my band? They were a real work of art. It looked like a professional did it. I hope you become very famous, Becca. Me, I'm going to become a famous dishwasher, nothing more. I play my guitar once in a while—just sit in my bedroom and pretend I'm James Taylor. You know, all folksy and feeling sorry for myself.

As far as your coming to visit me here—do you really think that Mom and Dad would let you? It doesn't seem very likely. It's just four of us guys living in this house, and no parents or anything, so don't get your hopes up.

Let me know how your mural goes. I'm sure you'll do great. Don't get mad at me if I don't write you again that soon. You know I'm not the greatest letter writer in the world. I just don't have that much to say.

Love,
Stevie

P.S. Don't worry about junior high. Nobody will make you take drugs.

I put the letter down. "Wow," said Kate. "He's really a good brother. You have no idea how lucky you are. You know what a bully Janette's brother is. The other day when I was over her house, her brother, Chris, hid a tape recorder under her bed and taped our whole conversation. That's all he does—plays with tape recorders and figures out how to bug rooms. It's disgusting; I hope he gets arrested."

Mom came into the room then. "Hi, girls," she said. "Did you find the cookies I left for you?"

"No," I said. "We were reading Stevie's letter first. Now we'll eat."

So we had our snack, and Mom sat down at the table with us, something she almost never did. "How are things at your house, Kate?" she asked.

"Okay," said Kate. "Dad's teaching. My mom is working on her book."

Mom looked out the window. "She must be very talented," she said. "It takes a lot to write a book."

"My mother says she doesn't know what she'd do if she didn't have her writing," Kate said. "She says that she'd be bored silly."

"I can understand that," said Mom. "Sometimes I get bored. When Stevie was here, it seemed that there was more to do—more people to look after and cook dinner for." Her voice trailed off, the way it often did lately.

Suddenly no one was talking anymore. Mom was looking at me. "You really miss Stevie, don't you?" she asked.

I nodded but couldn't say anything.

Mom folded her arms on the table. "It's been very upsetting for all of us, Becca," she said. "Even for your father."

"If it were Kate's dad, he wouldn't have acted like that!" I blurted out. "He would have made it easier for Stevie."

Kate looked embarrassed. "Well," Mom said quietly, "your father works very hard to make a nice home for us, and he loves you kids very much. Both of you."

"Mom," I said, because this was as good a time as any, "I want to go visit Stevie in the summer. I wrote and asked him if I could. I'll have enough money from the prize for the mural contest. I want to take a bus up to Montreal and stay with Stevie, even just for a week. Can I go?"

"That's a big decision," said Mom. "I'll have to discuss it with your father. But I'll tell you, Becca, I don't think he'll say yes."

"Why not?" I asked.

"There are a lot of reasons," she said. "Canada is very far away, you're twelve years old, there would be no adult supervision, and well, Dad is angry at Stevie. You know all that." Mom looked at the kitchen clock. "Oh, I have to go see if Susannah is still in her coma," she said. It took me a second, but then I realized that she was talking about a character on her favorite soap opera.

"I'd better get going, too," said Kate.

"I'll walk you home," I offered. I needed to get outside for a while.

Kate and I said goodbye in front of her house. "I'd invite you in," she said, "but my mom and dad are working today, and they want it really quiet. I'm not allowed to talk to them or anything."

I thought about her parents, sitting and concentrating really hard. Both of them wore round glasses that slipped down their noses. "See you tomorrow," I said.

"Okay," she said. Then she looked at me. "Don't be so sad," she said. "It makes me sad, too. Think about the good things."

Kate went into her house, and I began to walk home. I thought about standing in the auditorium holding a big paintbrush, dripping bright blue paint down onto a dropcloth. I saw myself making bold strokes with the brush. And then I saw the mural finished and everyone clapping. And then I saw the end of school, and the beginning of summer, and me traveling on a Greyhound bus up to Canada. I wouldn't be an elementary school student anymore. I would be about to start junior high. Thinking about all of this, I suddenly felt good. I turned the corner onto Marsha Lane and broke into a run.

CHAPTER 10

I'VE ALWAYS BEEN AFRAID OF HEIGHTS. WHEN I WAS very little, I was scared to walk down the stairs if there wasn't a banister. But now I stood at the top of a ladder and looked down at the floor. It seemed very far away, but I didn't really get dizzy, the way I thought I would.

It was weird to look at things from so high up. This was what it would be like to be a giraffe, I thought. I held a pencil in my hand and began drawing right on the auditorium wall. I was going to start with the faces, then do the bodies, then the sky, and save the flags for last, because I knew they were very hard to draw.

School had ended for the day, and now the only people left were some teachers, a couple of kids who had detention, the cast of the spring play, the janitor, and me. I could hear the janitor wheeling his trash barrel down the hallway. He had to go into every classroom and sweep up the spitballs from the floor.

In a minute the cast of the play came into the auditorium. They were headed by Mr. Canzoni, the favorite teacher in school. He was very young and handsome. He had a big black mustache that he twirled a lot when he spoke. He had written the spring play himself. It was called *The Story of Electricity*.

The actors took their places. I stood behind my screen, up on the ladder, a perfect place to watch. A very little girl held up her script and began to speak. "Oh. Oh. Oh," she said. "It is very dark in this room. Time to light another candle." She walked over to the left side of the stage and lit an imaginary candle.

Then a boy came up to her and said, "I'm sick and tired of having to light candles all the time. The light is never bright enough, and I need to study at night."

"Okay!" Mr. Canzoni called from the audience. "That was fine. Joanie, be sure to speak up. Now let's try the scene with Benjamin Franklin. Keith, are you ready?"

A boy named Keith came onstage. He was short and had bright red hair and freckles. He looked nothing like Benjamin Franklin! I wondered if he would get to wear a bald wig during the performance. He stood there in the middle of the stage and faced forward.

"My name is Benjamin Franklin," he read from his script in a loud voice. "It is so boring here in the house today. It's just raining and storming outside. I can't go for a walk in the woods or anything. I know!" he said. "I think I will try an experiment. Where is that kite I built? Goes rummaging around in a box for the kite!"

"Whoa, wait a minute," said Mr. Canzoni from his seat. "That's a stage direction, Keith. You're not supposed to say that line." He laughed.

"Oh," said Keith. "Sorry."

I turned back to the mural, and in a minute I didn't even hear the actors rehearsing their play. I even forgot that I was standing several feet off the ground.

I worked for an hour, and then I decided that was enough for the day. I slowly climbed down and went home. It was strange to walk home from school when it was so dark outside. It wasn't really that cold anymore. Spring had started. The year had gone by so fast. Soon I would have to start making real plans for the summer. I hadn't brought up the subject of Canada with my father yet. I didn't want to get into a fight with him. Things were okay, just so long as we stayed away from the subject of Stevie. My dad was going out of his way to be nice to me.

"You know," he said, "I told all the guys at the office about you winning the contest. They all want me to take a Polaroid of the mural when it's done and bring it in so they can see."

And he had even increased my allowance by a dollar. Things were going pretty well. I spent almost no money at all now; it went right into my Canada piggy bank. The bank sat on my dresser. It was in the shape of a pig, and I had named it Wilbur, after the pig in *Charlotte's Web,* my favorite book when I was younger. It was the first book I had ever cried over. At the part where Charlotte, the spider, dies, I had wept so loudly that Mom had come into my room, thinking I had hurt myself.

"What is it, dear?" she had asked, all worried.

"Charlotte's dead!" I had wailed.

Now my Wilbur bank was getting stuffed with bills and coins. No more movies on Saturdays with Kate and Janette and Emma. "Isn't there anything we can do that's free?" I asked Kate, but it was really hard to come up with things. There was always the mall, but we would always want to buy french fries, or a string of love beads, or *something.*

I stayed home a lot now and did my homework on weekends. Kate would come over, and we would look through magazines together. "I hate the way these models look," said Kate. "They're so skinny! I never want to look like that."

The models had their hair piled up on top of their heads, and they wore short dresses and high heels. They looked very uncomfortable. I loved just wearing jeans and a polo shirt and sneakers every day after school. It always felt great to take off my dress and put on play-clothes. I wondered if I would still be able to do that when

I was a teenager. I heard that you had to look good all the time or boys wouldn't like you. It worried me.

One afternoon Mrs. Reynolds from around the corner called me up. "Hi, Becca," she said. "I was wondering if you'd be free to baby-sit for Bradley on Friday night."

"Sure," I said. "That would be great. Can I bring a friend?"

"Well, I don't see why not," Mrs. Reynolds said. "Assuming it's a girl!"

"It is," I said.

"That would be fine. We'll see you and your friend at seven then."

On Friday night Kate and I rang the Reynoldses' doorbell. It played the beginning of a song; I don't remember which one. Mr. Reynolds answered the door. He was holding his necktie in his hand.

"Hello there," he said. "Come on in. My wife is giving Brad a bath, and that's always a major activity around here." In the background I could hear shrieking and running water.

"Now stop that, Bradley, I mean it!" came Mrs. Reynolds's voice.

Kate and I tried not to laugh. Mr. Reynolds stood in the hallway in front of the mirror and knotted his tie. "Why don't you girls go make yourselves at home?" he said. "My wife will be ready in a little while."

We sat down in the living room, on a very uncomfortable sofa. It had small, hard pillows on it and looked like it was out of a museum. In a minute there was a loud splash, and then four-year-old Bradley Reynolds came zooming down the hallway and into the living room. He was naked and very wet. Water spattered onto the rug. Mrs. Reynolds came running behind him with a towel.

"I don't want to get dry!" Bradley shrieked. "I want to stay wet!"

His mother stood there in the center of the room, holding the towel open at her side. She looked like a toreador holding a cape out to attract a bull. Bradley reluctantly walked over to his mother and let her wrap him in the big towel.

"Now please go back into the bathroom, sweetheart," she said. "You're ruining the nice carpet." Bradley ran back into the bathroom, humming the theme song from *Batman*.

"Hi, girls," Mrs. Reynolds said. "Forgive this little spectacle. I've got to go change right away, or we'll be late."

She went down the hall and came back fifteen minutes later, carrying her coat and purse. Mr. Reynolds looked at his watch. "All ready?" he asked, and Mrs. Reynolds nodded.

"We won't be home too late," she said. "The number of the restaurant is on the kitchen table. Also, the phone number of our pediatrician. Bradley's in his pj's, playing with his Hot Wheels cars. He can stay up for ten minutes more; then he simply must go right to sleep. One story, if he insists, but that's the limit. And no food at all. He shouldn't be a problem." Then they went out, leaving a cloud of Mrs. Reynolds's perfume behind.

Kate and I went down the hall to Bradley's bedroom. It had more toys in it than any room I'd ever seen. It was like being in a toy store. The floor was covered with trucks and cars, and the bed had a lot of stuffed animals on it. On the walls were big pictures of clowns and polar bears. There was a mobile hanging over his bed; four red sailboats bobbed in the air.

"Hi, Bradley," I said when I finally located him. He was lying underneath his bed, pushing a car out between the posts.

"Hi," he said, not looking up.

Kate sat down on the bed. "I've never seen so many objects in a room in my life," she said.

"My mother would have a clean attack," I said. "She'd want to go around the room with a vacuum and a garbage can."

Bradley made car sounds and talked to himself a little. "Okay," he said. "Now we're going to go, Mac. Bye. Let's honk the horn. Beep-beep."

Finally he got tired and crawled out from under the bed. "I want a story," he said. "First I have to urinate. Then I want a story."

He looked so serious and sounded so grown-up that Kate and I burst out laughing. "Okay," I said. "Go to the bathroom, and then I'll read you a story."

He came back a second later. "I couldn't go," he said. "But can I still have a story?"

So he climbed into bed, and I read him a book called *The Snowy Day*. At the end of it Bradley's eyes were closed and his mouth was open. I pulled the blanket around him, shut off his lamp, and then Kate and I tiptoed out of his room, stepping carefully over cars and trucks.

We went and sat in the Reynoldses' den. There was a big color TV set, and we watched *Love, American Style* for a while, then shut it off. Kate went into the kitchen and brought back an armful of food: Cheez Doodles, Pop Tarts, a bottle of soda.

She plopped down across from me on the couch and put the food on the coffee table. We ate for a while without talking. "What are you going to do when school lets out?" I asked her.

"I don't know," she said. "Dad told me about this science program at the university. It's for kids only, and you do experiments and get to see what it's like to work in a real lab. It sounds pretty neat."

"How long is it for?" I asked.

"A month," said Kate. "But it's only twice a week. This way you could go off to Canada for a week, and then we could spend the rest of the summer together. I don't feel like going away or anything. We could just go to the town pool and hang around or something. It would be fun."

"Our last summer before junior high school," I said. "It feels so weird to think about. Life in junior high school is very different. Nobody looks after you. You have to take care of yourself. You have eight different classes to go to all day. The bells ring, and you have four minutes to get to the next class."

"But the school is so big," said Kate. "What if you get lost and you're late for class?"

"Then they give you something called a pink slip," I said.

"I don't like the way junior high sounds," said Kate. "I don't want eight classes. I know Miss Brodskey isn't the nicest teacher in the world, but at least she knows your name. How could the teachers in junior high school memorize everybody's name? They have hundreds of students coming in and out."

"I guess they can't," I said. I was getting depressed about it.

"And what about drugs?" she asked. "Do you think you really can't go to the girls' room during the day? What if you really have to go? Do you think the teachers would let us use the teachers' bathroom?"

"Stevie said that's a lie," I said. "He said that nobody makes you take drugs. Somebody made that up."

"That's good to know," said Kate. "That movie in school was scary. But I know that Mom and Dad have smoked pot a couple of times. They just get silly and eat a lot."

"Like us," I said, looking around at all the food on the coffee table.

"Sometimes," said Kate, "I think I never want to start junior high. It would be easier to stay twelve forever."

"Yeah," I said. "I know what you mean. I think about Stevie. Just because he's nineteen, all these bad things happened to him. I don't think I ever want to be that old—everything changes."

"Oh, it won't be like that," Kate said, "because you're a girl. You won't have to go fight in a war."

"But I don't think *anybody* should have to," I said. "Not even boys." And as I said it, I knew that it was true, even though it wasn't what my parents thought.

"Me, either," said Kate. We sat together, crunching on Cheez Doodles. Our fingertips were turning bright orange.

"Becca?" she asked after a while.

"Yeah?"

"Do you think that even with all the work we'll have to do, and there being so many new kids, we'll still be good friends in junior high school?"

I looked at her. "Of course," I said. "Don't you?"

She looked worried. "I hope so," she said. "We're so much alike. I mean, we *think* alike a lot of the time. I never want that to stop. It's just that you're getting so much attention now, with the mural contest and everything. I just hope that you won't forget about me when you become a famous artist."

"First of all," I said, "I'm not going to become famous—at least, not for a long time anyway. And you're my best friend, Kate! How could you think I would ever forget about you?"

"I just get this way," she said. "You do everything well. Sometimes I think that I'm not interesting enough." She twisted her braid around in her hands. It was getting very long. Soon it would reach all the way down below her waist.

"I don't know what I would have done if you weren't around this year," I said. "How could I have gotten through the whole mess with Stevie and my family? I wouldn't have had anyone to talk to about it."

"I guess that's true," said Kate, and she began to cheer up.

All of a sudden we heard a sound coming from down the hall. It was Bradley. "No! No!" he shouted.

Kate and I ran into his bedroom. What if something terrible had happened, and we had just been sitting there talking, not paying attention? We got to the door of his room and looked in. Bradley was lying in bed, the covers all tangled up. He was fast asleep, having a nightmare. "Just stop that!" he was saying to some imaginary monster. He was only four years old, just a little boy. In a minute he relaxed; the nightmare ended by itself, but Kate and I still stood there, looking at him in the dim light of the room.

CHAPTER 11

THE MORE I WORKED ON THE MURAL, THE EASIER IT BE-
came. I was more sure of myself now, and I painted in
bigger strokes. I slashed bright red across the wall and
turned it into a boy's shirt. Everything was working out
fine. Every few days I would stand back and take a look
at the mural from far away, and I was always amazed
at what I saw. It really looked professional! The people
in the parade really seemed to be marching forward. I
would be done very soon.

A couple of kids peeked behind the screen when they

weren't supposed to, but I never minded. They always said nice things about my work. Even though the auditorium was kept locked, I was sure that other kids managed to sneak in and take a peek when no one was around.

I stayed after school every day now, and sometimes I even painted during lunch hour. The only person who ever came and watched me paint was Kate. She was the only one I wanted there. She got special permission from the cafeteria lady to bring her lunch tray into the auditorium. I told the cafeteria lady that I needed Kate to help me clean my brushes. She really believed me.

One afternoon I decided to go home right after school instead of staying to paint. I had gotten a lot done during lunch that day. I wanted to talk to Dad that night about going to Canada. It was time to bring the subject up, and I was very nervous.

Mom was vacuuming and didn't hear me come in. My snack was right there on the table, waiting for me. I ate it quickly, and then I sat there for a while longer. I was thinking about Stevie, like always. I got up and went into the living room, where the vacuum was still roaring away. Mom was bending down, poking the vacuum behind the couch. I heard a clink as a coin got sucked up. You could probably make a fortune, emptying out vacuum cleaner bags.

"Hi!" I shouted, but she didn't hear me. "Hi!" I shouted even louder, and this time she looked up.

She shut off the switch. "Oh, hello, Becca. I didn't hear

you come in over the vacuum noise." Her face was flushed.

"Mom," I said, "I've got to go visit Stevie. Please help me convince Dad. I think I'm going to bring it up at dinner tonight."

"Tonight?" she asked. "Oh, this is just going on and on, isn't it?"

I didn't know what to say to her. She just stood there holding the vacuum cleaner. "Would you help me?" I asked. "I mean, would you at least *talk* to Dad about it?"

"Becca," she said, "please don't put me on the spot like this. I'm caught right in the middle. I can't stand it anymore." She put her hand up to her eyes for a second, like she was very tired. Then she kicked on the switch of the vacuum cleaner and bent down to clean behind the couch. The conversation was over.

Dad came home from work at five-thirty. I was in my room, and I heard him come in. I went downstairs into the living room, where he had just sat down to read the newspaper.

"Hello there, Beccaroo," Dad said. "Did you have a good day at school?"

"It was fair to middling," I said. It was one of Dad's favorite expressions.

He smiled. "How's the painting going?" he asked. "I see you have a little bit of blue on the side of your nose."

I reached up and touched my nose. "Here?" I asked.

"No," said Dad. "Here." He touched my face, but nothing came off. "I guess you'll just have to scrub it off in the shower," he said.

I sat down on the footstool, and Dad picked up the folded newspaper. He looked through the main section, then turned to the business page. "Can I have some of the paper?" I asked him.

"Sure," he said, and he leafed through to find me the TV page, which I always read very carefully. Sometimes I would underline the shows I wanted to be sure to watch that night.

"No," I said, stopping him. "Can I have the news section?"

Dad looked surprised. "Sure," he said again, and he handed me the front part of the paper. He continued reading the business page, running his finger down the columns and squinting at the tiny numbers.

I began to read the headlines. They were all about Vietnam, like every day; only I had never paid too much attention before. There were a lot of things I didn't understand and a lot of words I had never seen before, but I got the point: The war was still going strong. Vietnam was a terrible place to be right now.

I turned the page and was face-to-face with a big photograph of a girl. She was running toward the camera, and she looked like she was crying. The caption said that she was Vietnamese, and her village was being bombed. She looked younger than me even. Maybe she was eleven at the most.

I just sat there looking at the picture. I couldn't stop. It was only when Mom came into the living room to say that dinner was ready that I finally put the newspaper down. But even then the girl's face stayed in my mind.

It was like a song that you can't get out of your head, but much worse. It was like a *terrible* song, something you hate, something that scares you.

When I was little, there was a commercial for steel wool that terrified me. The song scared me every time I heard it, and I don't really know why. It was supposed to be silly. There was a little steel wool pad singing in a high-pitched voice. It opened its mouth and sang, "Cleano gets your cookware spanking clean. Try it for yourself tonight and find out what I mean!" And then the steel wool pad burst into giggles. I used to run from the room shrieking, whenever that commercial came on TV.

We sat down to eat, and Mom and Dad began to talk about how much it would cost to get the leaky roof fixed. "I'll get an estimate tomorrow," said Dad.

I ate my dinner, but the girl's face was right there, and she was running toward me, as though she wanted me to save her.

"Becca," said Mom, "wasn't there something you wanted to talk about with your dad?"

I looked up, surprised. "Oh, yeah," I said. I wasn't ready; I hadn't had time to think about how I should say it. Mom and Dad were both looking at me expectantly. I took a deep breath. "Well," I said, "I've been thinking about the summer and wondering how I should spend it. I decided that I don't want to sit around the house the whole time, like a lot of kids do."

Dad smiled. "The answer is yes," he said.

I was shocked. "What?" I said. "Really?"

"Sure," said Dad. "I don't see why not. I know that money is kind of tight, and it's past the deadline, but maybe we could work it out. I'll call tomorrow."

"What do you mean?" I asked. It didn't sound like we were talking about the same thing.

"Skylark, of course," said Dad. "Isn't that it? Weren't you asking if you could go back this summer?"

"No," I said, and I looked down at my plate. This was going to be even harder than I had thought. I paused, then looked right at my father. "Dad," I said, "I want to take a bus to Canada to visit Stevie. Even if it's just for a week. I'll be getting a hundred dollars from the mural contest."

Dad shook his head. "No," he said. "I'm sorry, Becca, I can't allow it." He picked up his fork and continued eating.

"Dad!" I said. "You can't just say no like that! At least listen to me first!"

"There's nothing to listen to," said Dad. "Harriet, would you pass me the butter? Thank you."

"I'm going to be a teenager soon," I said. "A *teenager*. Old enough to make choices."

"And your brother was old enough to make choices, too," said Dad. "But that doesn't mean that they were the right ones!"

I was so frustrated that I just burst into tears. Mom and Dad sat there and watched me. Mom looked very concerned, but she didn't know what to do. So I sat in my chair and cried for a minute, and when I was done, I wiped my eyes with the napkin that was spread open on my lap.

"It's not fair," I said. "Nothing is. Just because I'm young, you think you can boss me around. It's the same with Stevie and the war. It's just not fair."

"Now calm down," Dad said. "Just calm down, miss. You are my daughter, and I think I know what is best for you. I do a lot to keep things happy and secure in this house. I buy you all the record albums you want, and I put up with the Beatles screaming in my ear every night, and I try to make things pleasant around the house. But you're being very difficult." He paused. "Look, Becca," he said, "you're only twelve years old, too young to go unchaperoned to Canada. I'd be happy to send you off to camp again, which is an appropriate thing for you to do."

"It's my money!" I said. "It's my money, and I can do what I want with it!"

"Becca," said Dad, "I had a hard day at work, and I'm very tired. I just want to eat the rest of my dinner peacefully. Can we drop the subject for the time being?"

So I didn't say another word about it at dinner, but I was still very upset. Mom looked at me as though to say, "I'm sorry, but what can I do?"

I finished my dinner and went upstairs, leaving Mom with all the dishes to wash. In my bedroom I reached into my jeans pockets and took out the money I had made baby-sitting the other day. I went to put it in my piggy bank; someday it would be spent on *something*. I was so upset that when I reached for the bank, it slid from my hands and dropped to the floor with a crash. The bank split open like a piñata—one of those Mexican toys filled with candy—and money spilled all over the floor. Now everything was a mess.

The next day at lunchtime Kate brought her tray into the auditorium. She already knew how upset I was; we had talked about it on our way to school in the morning.

I had finished painting all the people marching and was almost done with the sky as well. It was a cartoon blue, and I painted in a couple of soft clouds overhead. The only things left to do were the flags. I'm not too good at painting things evenly, and I knew that with flags you had to make sure that all the stars were the same size and you had room to fit them all in. I wasn't sure I would be able to get it right. And something else worried me, too. I wasn't even sure I *wanted* to paint flags anymore.

"What do you mean?" Kate asked when I told her. "That's what you planned. That's half of what you won for—because Mr. Cable liked your idea. I mean, I know that you don't feel very patriotic, and I don't blame you, but you can't just change it now, at the very end."

"I know," I said, but I put my paintbrush down in a tray and sat down on the bottom rung of the ladder. I rested my chin in my hand.

"You're just upset because of what happened last night," said Kate. "Because your father won't let you go to Canada."

"That's not it," I said. "I *am* very upset about that, but Stevie's letter made me think about a lot of things, too. It made me want to *do* something."

"Like what?" asked Kate.

"I don't know," I said. "It's like the time I didn't stand up for the pledge. I guess I shouldn't have won this contest, the way I feel now. They should have let somebody else paint the mural."

"You're the best artist in school, Becca," Kate said.

"Maybe I am," I said. "But even so, I'm hardly the most patriotic."

"What are you going to do?" asked Kate.

"I'm not sure," I said. "I'm not going to do anything more today. I'm just going to leave it overnight and think about it. Tonight I'm baby-sitting at the Reynoldses' again, even though it's a school night. They're just going to an early movie. Do you want to come?"

"Thanks," said Kate, "but I can't. I told Mom I would proofread her book. She's finished the first draft."

The bell rang, and lunch hour was over. We brought our trays back into the cafeteria and then went into class. "How is your mural going, Becca?" Miss Brodskey asked me, and I lied and told her it was going fine.

What I should do came to me that night. I was just sitting in the Reynoldses' den, trying to do my math homework for a change. I didn't understand anything, so I put the book down and turned on the color TV. It was a news show, and hundreds of faces crowded the screen.

"In Washington today," said the announcer, "peace demonstrators filled the Capitol steps in another protest against the war in Vietnam."

I looked at all the people, all the bright colors, all the long hair, and all the signs. The peace symbol was everywhere—on posters, on shirts, on buttons. There were even little kids in the crowd, babies strapped to their parents' backs. One baby had a yellow balloon tied to its arm, and there was a peace symbol drawn right on the balloon.

That was when it hit me. I could do something special with the mural. I could let everyone know how I felt. I was suddenly scared, but also very excited. I couldn't wait to continue painting. All at once I knew exactly what I was going to do.

The next day Kate came over to me in the cafeteria. "Do you want me to come with you while you paint today?" she asked.

"Um, I think I want to be alone, if that's okay," I said to her. "But I need to see you as soon as school lets out, all right?"

"Well, all right," said Kate, but she looked hurt. She brought her tray to the back of the room and sat down with Emma and Janette.

I carried my own tray down the hall and looked doubtfully at today's menu. Chow mein—some thick, clear stuff with a couple of pieces of celery and chicken floating around—a carton of lukewarm milk, and an apple, the only thing that looked edible.

I went into the silent auditorium and put my tray down. I picked up the apple and turned it over and over in my hands. Then I went and moved the screen from my mural, so I could see what my work looked like from far away. That's how you're supposed to look at art.

Mr. and Mrs. Ruskin took me and Kate into New York City once, and we went to a museum. They showed us something called a pointillist painting; it was made up of little dots of paint. "I don't get it," I had said, peering closely at the picture. It didn't look like anything to me.

"Stand back," said Mrs. Ruskin, and I walked a few feet backward and looked again. All the dots seemed to have joined together. Suddenly I could see a lady holding an umbrella, and then trees, and water. It was fantastic!

So now I walked all the way to the other side of the auditorium and looked at my mural. It was almost ready, except for the flags. Could I really go ahead with what I wanted to do? I thought about it for a long moment. Yes, yes, I could. I simply had to.

I went over to the ladder and knelt down. I took out the wooden stick I had been using every day, and I began to stir up the can of red paint. I felt like a witch making some kind of secret brew. I dipped the brush into the paint, and then I began. I painted bright red peace symbols on all the flags—big, round circles with upside-down Y's in them. My heart was pounding. I knew I would get into big trouble for this, but I suddenly didn't care.

All of a sudden I heard a sound behind me. The doors of the auditorium opened. I peered behind the screen. It was Mr. Canzoni, the drama coach.

"Hi there," he said. "I know it isn't allowed, but can I take a peek?"

"Well, uh . . ." I said, and I was very nervous, but I couldn't say anything more. Mr. Canzoni was striding toward me. He walked behind the screen and looked up. He stood there with his arms crossed. He didn't say anything for the longest time. Finally he whistled, very low. "Wow," he said. "This is quite a surprise." He looked at me. "Does anyone else know about these peace symbols?" he asked me.

"No," I said in a tiny voice. "I just painted them."

I thought that Mr. Canzoni would yell at me or tell me he would have to "report me to the authorities," like they said on TV. But all he did was smile.

"Don't worry," he said. "I won't say anything. But it should be interesting to see what kind of reaction you get at the assembly tomorrow morning."

I tried to smile, too, but the corners of my mouth wouldn't go up. I stood there, dripping red paint all over the dropcloth on the floor. Mr. Canzoni walked across the auditorium to the doors.

"Good luck!" he called out to me, and his voice echoed in the empty room.

PART THREE

CHAPTER 12

THE SPRING ASSEMBLY WAS HELD ON A PERFECT FRIDAY morning. First there was going to be a talk, and then my mural would be unveiled in front of the entire school. We all filed into the auditorium and sat down. Kate was on one side of me, and Miss Brodskey was on the other side. I was going to be presented with the $100 prize onstage. I would have to walk up, shake hands with Mr. Cable, pick up my check, then go sit down again.

I was very nervous, and I had reason to be. Only Kate and Mr. Canzoni knew why. Kate squeezed my hand tightly, giving me reassurance. The mural was hidden behind the screen. The last colors had barely dried. Two fifth-grade boys stood on either side of the screen, ready to move it whenever Mr. Cable gave them the signal.

The talk in the assembly was being given by an astronaut. He didn't come onstage wearing a space suit, though, which was kind of disappointing. You just had to take his word for it that he really was an astronaut. He was actually kind of short, but he had a nice smile. He took questions from the audience after he had finished speaking.

"Yeah, like, what do you do if you're in a rocket wearing your space suit and you have to go to the bathroom?" Tommy Vesco asked. Everybody snickered.

The astronaut answered, and then a second grader asked if girls could ever become astronauts. The questions went on for a while, but I didn't really listen that closely. I was worrying about my mural.

Finally Mr. Cable returned to the microphone, and the astronaut left. "Now, boys and girls," said Mr. Cable, "we have come to the final part of our program today. As you all know, the school mural has been completed and will be unveiled so we can all see the artwork of our prize-winner, Rebecca Silverman." He cleared his throat. "Before we remove the screen from the mural," he said, "I'd like to call Rebecca up onstage to present her personally with her check for a hundred dollars. Rebecca?" He looked out into the audience, and I stood up. Kate swung her legs to the side so I could walk by. Everybody was quiet as I walked onto the stage. My heart was thumping. It felt weird to know that everyone was looking at me.

I stood next to Mr. Cable, and he towered over me. Even the microphone towered over me. Mr. Cable took a long white envelope from the inside pocket of his suit. "On behalf of the Board of Education," he said, "I'd like to present you with this check and our heartiest congratulations. This mural means a lot to us in these troubled times. We at the Thomas Jefferson Elementary School believe in the words 'My Country, 'Tis of Thee.' " He stopped speaking and looked out over the auditorium. There were so many faces staring back.

"And now," said Mr. Cable, "if the monitors will please remove the screen, we can all have a first look at Rebecca Silverman's work of patriotic art."

The two boys folded up the screen, bringing my mural into view. It certainly was bright. The colors looked stronger than ever. There it was: a parade of marchers smiling and carrying flags. The peace symbols glowed. They looked huge, much bigger than I thought they would look. They practically jumped out of the wall at you.

Everyone just stared. A couple of people whispered. Nobody clapped, like they were supposed to. The teachers began to talk. In a minute the whole auditorium was buzzing.

Mr. Cable turned to me, and his face was dark with anger. "Rebecca!" he said. "What have you done? You were supposed to paint American flags!"

I tried to answer, but I found that I couldn't even speak.

"Quiet!" said Mr. Cable into the microphone. "Please, boys and girls, let's have some quiet."

In a moment the ripple of talk stopped, and the room was still. "Now," said Mr. Cable, "Rebecca's mural has come as quite a . . . surprise . . . to us. I had no idea that she was planning to paint peace symbols in this room. The original idea was that the figures marching would be carrying American flags. Isn't that right, Rebecca?" he asked, turning to me.

I nodded. I just wanted to jump off that stage and run out of the auditorium. I wanted to keep running until I couldn't run anymore.

"Now I'd like to end the assembly here," said Mr. Cable. "Will you all please line up and go back to your classrooms in an orderly fashion?" The kids started to get up and leave, and Mr. Cable turned to me. "Rebecca," he said, "will you please come to my office immediately?" And then he wheeled around and marched down off the stage, still carrying the white envelope.

Mr. Cable went up to Miss Brodskey and whispered something to her. She nodded and turned to look at me. There was a tight, serious expression on her face. I caught a glimpse of Kate just as she was about to walk out the door. She was looking at me, and her eyes were very wide. She seemed to be sending me some sort of message, only the connection was bad and I couldn't make it out. Even our ESP wasn't working now. I was on my own.

I had been in the principal's office only once before, and that was just to deliver a message. I was never one of the kids sitting by the plants against the windows, waiting to be yelled at. I never thought I would find myself there, but here I was. In a minute another kid came and sat down next to me.

"What did you do?" I asked him, like we were in jail.

"Tripped my enemy on the way out of the auditorium," he said. He looked at me. "You're Becca, right?" he asked. I nodded. "You're famous," he said. "That was something, those peace symbols. Far-out! Everyone was whispering about it. Far-out!"

A few minutes later Mr. Cable appeared in front of us and motioned for me to step into his office. It was a small, bright room with a poster on the wall that said, "Sock It to Me." Mr. Cable sat down behind his desk, and I sat down on a wooden chair across from him. I was terrified.

"Rebecca," said Mr. Cable, clasping his hands together, "do you understand the seriousness of what you have done?"

I thought about this. "No," I finally said. "I guess not."

Apparently that wasn't the right answer. "Well, let me explain it to you then," said Mr. Cable. "You were given the honor of being chosen to paint the school mural. You deliberately deceived us by pretending that you were going to paint something very different. That is not just poor judgment, Rebecca. That is lying." He stopped, out of breath. "Now, what are we going to do about this?" he asked.

I didn't say anything. I sat and looked at my hands. There were little bits of paint under my fingernails. Finally Mr. Cable sent me back to class, but he told me that we were certainly not finished talking. As I walked out the door, the kid by the windows whispered to me, "Did you get twenty years of hard labor?"

When I came back into the classroom, everyone looked up. Miss Brodskey was standing at the blackboard, writing, "*I before E, except after C.*" I sat down at my desk; everyone looked at me and poked one another.

Kate passed me a note immediately. I held it in the palm of my hand and read it. "Dear Becca," it read, "are you okay? I was so worried about you that I didn't know what to do. I will stick by you 4-ever. Your best friend, Kate."

I crunched the letter up and tried to smile at Kate. I was so glad that she was there, that she had moved in, that she sat next to me, that she was my friend. I just wanted to hug her and maybe even cry for a minute. But I couldn't do any of that, because it was the middle of class.

I opened my notebook and tried to concentrate on the lesson, but I was very shaken up. Later on in the morning the classroom intercom buzzed, and Miss Brodskey went and spoke into the receiver. "Yes?" she said. "Oh? Very well, we'll be there." I knew that it was about me.

Sure enough, during independent study, Miss Brodskey came to my desk and told me that Mr. Cable wanted to see me again right after school. This time, she said, he wanted her to be there also.

During lunch hour everyone crowded around me and asked questions, but I sipped my milk and didn't say very much.

"Hey," said Tommy Vesco, "I've got to hand it to you, Becca. That was pretty neat, what you did."

And then I realized something: I may have been in trouble, but a lot of the kids in school seemed to be really impressed by what I had done. A couple of kids walked by me and made peace signs with their hands. I made the peace sign back. Soon the whole cafeteria was doing it. The cafeteria lady stood in the middle of the room, looking bewildered.

But I got through the afternoon meeting all right. It was hard at first. Miss Brodskey and Mr. Cable sat and looked at me, waiting for me to explain myself. And then I just began to talk. I told them the story about Stevie and everything that had happened that year. I told them about Stevie's letters to me and how they had started me thinking. I talked about the photograph in the newspaper.

"I didn't plan to paint the peace signs all along," I said. "I just decided to do it at the last minute. Everything built up, I guess."

We sat in silence for a while, and then Miss Brodskey said something amazing. "I think it's admirable," she said, "that such a young person has made a stand."

Mr. Cable looked stunned. "Yes . . . well . . ." he said.

"I do think it was wrong of Becca not to stick to her original plans for the mural," Miss Brodskey said. "But I don't think she ought to be punished."

Mr. Cable sighed. "This is a very difficult matter," he said. "I'm not sure what ought to be done about it."

So we sat in silence for a little while longer, and finally Mr. Cable decided that I wouldn't be punished. He reached into his jacket pocket and handed me the white envelope with the check in it. My peace symbols would have to be painted over, he said. He would have the art teacher, Mrs. Green, turn them into American flags.

Mr. Cable called up my mother that afternoon and talked to her about the matter. "What are we going to do with you?" Dad asked me during dinner.

I shrugged. "You know," said Dad, "you're becoming just like your brother—rebellious already, and you're only twelve. I just don't understand."

Still, I didn't say anything. I sat and looked down at my plate. "Becca, you're turning into an independent young lady," Dad said, and for a minute there I couldn't tell what his tone of voice was: Disappointed? Proud? Sad?

My parents and I sat at the dinner table, and I looked across at the empty chair facing me. Skipper walked around below, looking for food. I felt his warm tongue flick against my ankle. I reached down and scratched him behind the ears. Then I looked at my father.

"Dad?" I said. "If I'm so independent, then why can't I go visit Stevie in Canada this summer?"

"Becca," Dad said in a tired voice, "you never quit, do you?"

After dinner Dad went into the living room to watch TV, and Mom and I stayed in the kitchen, cleaning up. Mom didn't talk to me, like she usually did. She was very distracted tonight. She stood at the sink washing dishes, but she had a funny expression on her face.

"Mom?" I said. "Are you okay?"

She turned to me, a plate in her hand. "Would you dry this, please?" she asked me, as though I hadn't spoken to her. I reached for the plate, but before I could take it, she had dropped it to the floor. It landed with a loud crash, startling us both.

"Oh," she said in a small voice. "I'll get the broom."

She was very upset, I realized. It wasn't about breaking the plate; it was about *me*. It was about what had happened to our family. She came back with the broom, but I could tell she didn't want to talk. We finished up the work together, neither of us saying anything.

After the kitchen was clean, I went up to my bedroom, and Mom went into the living room. The TV was shut off, and I could hear Mom and Dad talking. I couldn't make out what they were saying, and I continued to do my homework. "Explain the basic concepts of the Declaration of Independence," Miss Brodskey had written on the ditto. Oh, no. That was going to take some thinking.

I sat there at my desk and didn't even hear my father come up the stairs. The next thing I knew there was a knock at my door. "Come in," I called, and I turned around.

Dad poked his head in. "Am I disturbing you?" he asked.

"Just finishing up," I said, and he came into the room.

Dad looked too big to be in my room—like Alice in Wonderland, after she's swallowed the bottle of stuff that makes her grow. The only light on now was my desk lamp. The room had that dark, mysterious look about it that I liked so much.

"Can I sit down?" Dad asked, and I said, "Sure." He sat down awkwardly on the edge of my bed. He looked around, as though he had never been here before, as though it weren't his house. But then I realized that Dad had almost never spent any time in my room. I guess he thought it was girls' territory, and he wasn't wanted. The only times he ever really came in was to close the windows late at night when it had begun to storm and I was half-asleep.

"I've been downstairs talking with your mother," said Dad. "We were talking about you."

"Oh," I said.

Dad picked up the snowstorm paperweight from my bedside table and shook it. Snow fell heavily over the village inside. I sometimes used to lie in bed and hold the paperweight in my hands, wondering what it would be like to live inside that round glass world.

Dad put it back down and folded his arms. "This has

been quite a year for all of us," he said.

"I know," I said.

"We've all been under stress," he said. "I made certain decisions, and I stuck to them. I still think I was right, Becca. Sometimes I stay up at night, wondering."

I had never thought about my dad not being able to sleep. I always imagined him dropping right off, snoring away. "All I know," said Dad, "is that I have to stick to what I believe. When I fought in World War Two, I felt very proud to be able to serve my country. And now," he said, "here I am, years later, still in one piece. A lot less hair, though." He reached up and touched his head.

He stopped for a moment and looked seriously at me. "What I want to say to you, Becca," he said, "is that I'm going to try to make things a little less stressful around here. I don't want you to think of me as some kind of villain. I'm always the one who has to say no."

This was the longest talk that my dad and I had ever had. I felt like crying, and I wasn't sure why.

"Your mom is pretty upset," said Dad. "She never gets like this. She just wants some *peace* in the house again. She wants things to be normal." He paused. "She told me to come up here and talk to you," he said. He looked down at the floor, then sighed.

"She thinks it wouldn't be such a crime to let you go to Canada," he mumbled.

I looked up sharply. "Really?" I said. I crossed my fingers. Oh, please, I thought. Let it be true. Please. I want this more than anything.

"It's hard for me to watch you grow up," said Dad.

"Sometimes it makes me feel very old. And the house always feels so big with you gone. All those summers, when you and Stevie went off to Skylark, your mom and I would joke that the house wasn't messy enough. It didn't feel right, without sneakers and sketch pads left all over the floor. I guess I would feel that way if you went off to Canada. I would also feel worried," he said. "After all, you are a young girl, and Canada is very far away. But a week is a week." He sighed. "I'm still not sure that this is the right thing to do, but I'm going to do it anyway. I'm going to say yes."

I sprang up from my chair. "Oh, Dad!" I said.

I wanted to hug him then, but I didn't. We didn't ever touch very much. With my dad, you weren't really sure of where to put your arms. He wasn't too comfortable about being hugged. So we just stood there and smiled at each other for the longest time.

CHAPTER 13

THE NEXT DAY WAS SATURDAY, AND I WENT OVER TO Kate's house early in the morning. She answered the door herself. "Hi," she said. "This is a surprise. I thought you had to work on the Declaration of Independence thing all weekend."

"I do" I said. "But I have to tell you something incredible."

"What is it?" she asked. We still stood in the doorway.

"I'm going to Canada!" I said.

Kate's mouth opened. "Wow!" she said. Then we jumped up and down together, like two Mexican jumping beans.

"Come on in," said Kate, "and tell me everything. We have to be very quiet, though. Mom and Dad are really weird early in the morning these days." Just then Mr. Ruskin walked past us in a bathrobe, carrying two cups of coffee. He didn't even say hello.

Kate and I went into her bedroom together. Her bed was unmade, and there were clothes lying all over the floor. It always amazed me that Kate's mom didn't care if she cleaned up or not.

"Here," said Kate, pulling the cover over the bed. "Sit down and tell me what happened."

So I told her the story of what had happened last night. "See, your dad's not so bad after all," Kate said. "It all worked out in the end."

I leaned back against the wall and closed my eyes. I began to picture myself in Montreal. I would speak French, which I would learn instantly, and everybody would think I was really Canadian. I began to daydream, and Kate's voice pulled me back.

"Becca," she said, "I'm really going to miss you."

"You'll have a great time while I'm gone," I said. "It's only a week. You'll have that science program, and the pool, and your parents. You can spend a lot of time with them."

Kate looked annoyed all of a sudden. "You know," she said, "you have this really warped view of my parents.

You think my family is the greatest thing in the world. Well," she said, "it's not!" Kate sat up in bed and hugged her knees tightly. "You forget that I'm an only child," she said. "I have to be alone a lot. My parents spend a lot of time together, and they close the door. Sometimes they forget that I exist. I know they're young and cool and everything, but sometimes things are really hard for me. You only notice the good stuff," said Kate.

I didn't know what to say. I had never thought about it like this before. "I'm sorry," I said in a tiny voice.

"You have the greatest brother," she said. "I know he's in Canada, but it's better than not having a brother at all. When I was six, I had an imaginary brother named Tropicana. I named him after the orange juice. We went everywhere together. Things get really lonely, Becca," she said. "Like now, my mom and dad are in their room, and I know that I can't burst in and talk to them. I like being at your house because at least you have a normal family. There's nobody walking around saying 'Shhhhhh' all the time. And those letters from your brother—I would give anything for a letter from someone who was my brother. You have somebody there who just knows everything about you. When we go on family vacations, I always have to sit in the back seat of the car by my-self. And I always get my own motel room, too. I get lonely a lot."

"Why didn't you say any of this before?" I asked Kate. I was astonished.

"I don't know," she said. "I guess because you had

enough problems with your own family. Mine felt like nothing compared with yours. But sometimes I get upset when you keep saying how perfect my parents are. They're not! I'm not even allowed to have a TV. And do you know that the first Yodel I ever tasted was at your house? Life isn't so great over here," said Kate. "You should trade places with me sometime; you'd see for yourself."

"Oh, Kate," I said. "I'm sorry."

"It's okay," Kate said after a second. "But I'm glad I told you how I felt; I couldn't keep it in any longer. The only thing that worries me now," she said, "is that you're going away. I'm going to be lonely again."

"It's just for a week," I said. "And then we'll have the rest of the summer together."

"Just promise me that you'll come home when the week is up," she said. "I don't want to get a telegram saying you're staying there with Stevie forever."

"I promise," I said.

Things were pretty good after that. Back at my house, Mom and Dad and I made plans for my trip. Mom talked to Stevie on the telephone, and he assured her that he would take good care of me. At the end of the conversation Mom handed me the phone.

"Hi," I said to Stevie. "Can you believe they're really letting me come?"

"I think it's great," said Stevie. "I hope you're not going to be bored out of your skull. I'll have to start planning things that we can do—"

"Stevie," I said, interrupting, "we don't have to *do* anything. I just want to spend time with you. I'm not a little kid anymore."

He laughed softly; I remembered that laugh very well. It sent a chill through me now. "I know you're not," he said. "I forget sometimes."

School was winding down to its final days, and I could barely pay attention. One day I was walking down the hall, and I passed by the auditorium. The doors were wide open. I stopped and stared. Inside, I could see Mrs. Green, the art teacher, standing in front of my mural. She had a couple of cans of paint next to her, and she was painting over the peace signs on my mural.

I walked into the auditorium. I watched for a moment as she slowly turned one of the peace signs into an American flag. I felt awful, but I couldn't stop looking.

"Mrs. Green?" I said.

She jumped, turned her head. "Oh, hi, Becca," she said.

There was a long, awkward pause.

We stood there looking at each other for a few seconds, and finally Mrs. Green put down her paintbrush. "Becca," she said, "I'm sorry to have to change your mural. But there was nothing I could do about it." She pushed her eyeglasses up higher on her nose.

"That's okay," I said, but still I just stood there.

Mrs. Green looked at her watch. "I have to get back to work on this," she said. "I hope you understand."

"Yeah," I said, but my voice came out tiny.

Mrs. Green dipped a brush in a can of white paint and continued painting stars. I watched as a whole field of them appeared, twinkling against a deep blue sky. Then I turned and left the room.

I always felt bad when I looked at the mural after that. But it didn't matter. Everyone remembered it the way it had first looked. Every day kids still made peace signs with their hands when they passed me in the hall. I was famous all over school. It was a pretty nice way to end the year.

It was cardigan weather now. I wore light spring dresses and knee socks to school and just grabbed the cardigan sweater that Mom insisted I take with me. At lunchtime we were allowed to go outside after we had finished eating. Kate and I lay down on the grass and looked up at the sky.

"When I'm studying science in college," she said, "I'll understand things like why the sky is blue and the grass is green. That's the kind of thing I've always wanted to know."

"And when I'm a painter," I said, "then I'll be able to paint it so it looks real."

There were shouts in the distance. A couple of kids were throwing a softball around. And from far away I could hear a group of little girls, maybe second graders, jumping rope. They sang songs, and the rope slapped against the blacktop in rhythm.

"Remember being eight years old and jumping rope?" I asked Kate.

"No," she said. "We didn't do that at my other school. We had Scream Time instead."

I suddenly missed jumping rope. I'd heard that in junior high school kids brought their guitars out onto the grass during lunch hour and played folk songs. Girls sat with their heads on boys' shoulders. I looked around the elementary school playground and realized that I would miss this place a lot. I liked seeing the Jungle-gym everyday, and the seesaws, even though I was getting too old to go on them.

The last day of school was warm and sunny. A lawn mower buzzed outside. While other classes had big, noisy parties that could be heard all the way down the hall, Miss Brodskey made us sit quietly at our desks while she passed out end-of-the-year presents. She walked from desk to desk, handing every kid a slim wrapped box. Finally she came to me. "Here you are, Becca," she said. "I hope you have a happy summer. Will you be going away at all?"

I looked up at her. I was still the only kid who really liked Miss Brodskey. She had stuck up for me in front of Mr. Cable. She may not have had a sense of humor, but she was really a nice person underneath.

"I'm going to visit my brother in Canada," I said.

"Well, that should be exciting," she said. "I hope you have a good time. It's been nice having you as my pupil."

I suddenly thought about Jessie Diggory, my favorite counselor, and I remembered the way she had told me what a good camper I was. When Miss Brodskey walked away, I opened my present. It was a box of pencils, with words printed on them in gold. "With Best Wishes from Your Teacher," it said on the side of each pencil.

Five minutes before the end of school Miss Brodskey gave out our report cards. I wasn't too worried; despite everything that had happened that year, I knew that I had done pretty well.

The bell rang, sounding louder and more final than ever. Elementary school was over for good! For once nobody raced out of their seats. We all sat there for a moment, watching Miss Brodskey. She sat behind her desk, her arms folded in front of her.

"Well, children," she said, "I'm sure you will all turn into fine young adults. Have a pleasant summer, all of you." And then Miss Brodskey smiled, something I had never seen her do before.

Kate and I walked out of class together. When we got into the hall, we linked arms. "This is really it," she said, and I felt a very strange feeling in my stomach. I looked around me for one final time. Kids flooded out of classrooms. Two boys lugged a big cage with a guinea pig in it. Classroom pets needed homes for the summer.

I said goodbye on the corner to everyone I liked. "I hear you're going to Canada," said Mitchell Sampson. "That's great."

"What are *you* doing this summer?" I asked him.

"Building a robot," he said. "Maybe it will be finished before the fall, and you could come see it."

"Okay," I said.

As Kate and I walked home, we opened our report cards and looked at them. "Not bad," we said to each other, peering over the other's shoulder to see.

We each went to our own house. I knew that Mom would be home and anxious to hear about the last day of school. And there she was, standing at the front door with Skipper. She waved to me as I came up the walk. "Hi, dear," she said, kissing me. "Congratulations. You're a seventh grader!"

I came into the house and sat down at the table with Mom, while she read my report card and I ate three brownies. "I'm so proud of you," said Mom. "You're very brainy, you know that?"

We had a long conversation in the kitchen. We began to plan my trip to Canada. We decided that I would leave a week from Monday. It would take an entire day for me to get there. I would bring my sketch pad on the bus, and a good book. Mom promised that she would pack me a lunch with lots of snacks in it. I was looking forward to the ride in a way.

Kate and I counted off the days. "Well," she said. "Four more to go, then blast-off. And when you're gone, I'm going to count the days until you come back, too."

"It's only seven," I said. "You won't even notice that I'm not around." But I knew that wasn't true. If Kate were the one leaving and I were the one staying, I knew that I would count the days, too. I would think about her a lot in Canada, I knew, but it was easier being the one who was going away.

The night before I left, I suddenly felt in the mood for an ice cream sundae. I called Kate up, and we met on the corner with our bikes, to ride out to the Dairy Queen. It was the first time I would be going there since Stevie left.

The night was warm, and crickets stuttered all around us. It was funny how you could never see them but only hear them. Kate and I rode in single file, and we shouted to each other during the drive.

"I want a brown bonnet!" said Kate.

"I want a double sundae!" I called back.

I did want ice cream, but I also wanted to see Nina, my brother's girl friend. I wanted to tell her that I was going to Canada. Maybe she had a message for me to give Stevie, or a present. I imagined her going to the back of the store and cutting off a piece of her hair for me to bring him. Something romantic like that.

Kate and I parked our bikes and began to walk up toward the Dairy Queen window. I could see Nina inside, wearing her uniform. She was standing by the ice cream machine, and she had her arm around a boy. He was tall and skinny, with long red hair. They were laughing over something.

I stopped and watched them for a second. "Kate," I said, "I don't think I'm really that hungry after all."

"What?" she asked. "But you said—" She cut her sentence short and looked where I was looking. "Ohhhhhh," she said, suddenly understanding. "We can forget it."

I loved Kate then for just knowing without having to be told. So we got on our bicycles and pedaled home in silence. I wasn't mad at Nina. I just felt a little bit sad. She and Stevie lived in different countries; they couldn't be expected to go steady forever. But I didn't feel like talking to Nina right then. I didn't want to know anything about her new boyfriend.

Kate and I said goodbye on my front porch. This was it; we would be apart for a whole week. A lot could happen in a week.

"Oh, Becca," Kate said as we stood under the porch light, "you're the best friend I ever had. You're so much better than any of the five kids in my other school. At first, when we moved here, I thought I was going to hate it, but you make up for everything."

We hugged for at least thirty seconds. Neither of us wanted to let go. "It's only a week," I said. "Then we'll be swimming at the town pool, and my mom will be on the side, playing Mah-Jongg with her friends."

"I know," said Kate. "I know. Oh, this is so dumb of me." She walked down the steps and picked up her bicycle from where it was leaning against the rail. "Have a fun trip," she said. "Bring me back some picture postcards."

I went into the house. The screen door slammed with a shudder behind me. Both my mom and dad were up, watching TV. The news was on, and there were pictures of people fighting. Vietnam, I knew. It just seemed to go on forever, this war.

"Are you all packed?" Dad asked me.

"Yeah," I said. I wasn't taking too much.

I don't know how I ever fell asleep that night. It took me the longest time, but finally I slept. I tossed and turned a lot though, twisting up the blankets.

In the morning it was raining, but warm outside. The air smelled like wet metal. Mom and Dad went with me to the Greyhound station. This time there were a lot of people getting on the bus for Canada. It wasn't like when Stevie left; it was summer now, and people were going on vacations.

Mom had taken my $100 check and bought me traveler's checks. That's like money, but nobody can use it if it's stolen. I took my suitcase onto the bus, and Dad helped me slide it onto the rack over my seat. Mom and Dad weren't supposed to be on the bus, but the driver let them on for just a minute before we were about to leave. I found a seat by the window, next to a nun.

"Excuse me, Sister," Mom said to the nun. "This is our daughter, and she is traveling alone for the first time. Do you think you would be able to look after her?"

The nun smiled. She had bright blue eyes and could have been very young or very old. "Of course," she said. "I'd be happy to."

Everyone else was sitting down, and Mom and Dad stood in the narrow aisle. It was almost time. "Well," said Dad, looking around nervously, "we'd better hop off, Harriet, before we end up as stowaways."

They each leaned across the seat and kissed and

hugged me. Dad was getting better at it.

"I'll be fine!" I said to them. I realized that I was much less nervous than they were, and I was the one going on the adventure.

Mom and Dad hurried off the bus and continued waving to me from the sidewalk. The nun smiled at me. "What an independent young lady you are," she said. "My."

Then she took out a Baggie of pistachio nuts and offered me some. We sat there, happily cracking nuts, and pretty soon I looked out the window and saw that we were on the highway, and all the signs said NORTH.

CHAPTER 14

THE BUS DRIVER'S VOICE CRACKLED OVER THE LOUD-speaker, waking me up. "In two minutes," he said, "we will be reaching our last stop, Montreal, Canada. I hope you have had a pleasant journey."

I sat up in my seat and looked out the window. It was very late at night, and the sky was black. The road looked like any other road. We had traveled for so long, stopping a couple of times at rest stops. Everyone on the bus was very nice, and we had all joked around. The nun, whose name was Sister Mary Claire, insisted on buying me a Coke from a soda machine, when we stopped at a gas station. She was very friendly the whole time. I asked her if she had ever watched *The Flying Nun* on TV, but she said no.

My leg fell asleep, and I had to shake it before it woke up again. It felt like it was filled with little stingers. I was suddenly very worried. What if Stevie wasn't there? What if I had traveled for fifteen hours and he had forgotten I was coming? I would be all alone in a strange bus station in a foreign country.

The bus pulled to a halt in a big, dark garage. Everybody stood up and stretched, then began reaching for their overhead luggage. A nice man across the aisle reached up and brought down my suitcase. "Here you are, young lady," he said. "Have a nice time in Montreal."

We walked off the bus. My body felt very light, like it might float away. All of a sudden we were in the bus terminal, and it looked like all the bus terminals I knew. I looked around the bright room. It was very late, but people were walking around, waiting to meet friends or to get on buses themselves. Maybe there was some little girl there who was going to go visit her brother in New York. There were a lot of people rushing around, but I didn't see Stevie. He wasn't here; he really wasn't. I was all alone in Canada.

Sister Mary Claire turned to me. "Do you see your brother?" she asked.

"No," I said, and my voice was very high, like I was

about to cry. I blinked back a tear, and when I opened my eyes again, I saw him. He was running toward me. His hair was wild—very long and full—and he was wearing a psychedelic sweat shirt, but it was him. It was Stevie.

"Becca!" he yelled.

We ran toward each other, and when he reached me, he swung me up into the air. My suitcase flew out of my hand. I hoped it didn't hit somebody.

Sister Mary Claire stood patiently nearby, and when I was finally able to separate from Stevie, she and I said goodbye. "It's been a very pleasant journey," she said. "God be with you."

I wondered if God was with me. All I knew was that Stevie was. He had his arm around me, and I could feel the dampness from the rain on his sweat shirt. He looked shaggy and tall; he seemed to have grown a few inches since I last saw him. His eyes were the same dark brown.

"My kid sister," he kept saying. "I can't believe my kid sister is here in exile with me."

He messed up my hair, the way he used to. We kept reaching out and tweaking each other's nose or tickling each other, as we walked out of the bus station. We were just so happy to see each other and so overexcited. I knew that we were in exactly the same mood.

Stevie pointed to a beat-up van in the parking lot. "That's us," he said. "It belongs to Michel, one of the guys I live with."

The van was orange and had peace signs painted on

the sides. I wanted to tell Stevie about the mural, but I thought I would wait. We climbed in. The van smelled like incense inside.

"PU," I said. "What's that?"

"Frangipane," Stevie said. "Michel burns it all the time. You'd better get used to it; the whole house smells like incense."

I sat next to my brother and looked at his profile as he drove. "Are you hungry?" he asked. "I'll cook you dinner when we get home."

It was a very short drive to the house. We pulled into a driveway in front of a rickety house. All the houses on the street looked old but sort of interesting. They all seemed different from each other, unlike the houses on Marsha Lane, which were exactly alike.

Inside, the house did smell like incense, but it also smelled like marijuana and old food. A cat was licking its paws in the hallway. It stopped, stared at us, then went back to what it was doing. "That's Jefferson," said Stevie, reaching down and scooping up the cat in his arms. "Named after the Jefferson Airplane."

We walked into the living room. There were big pillows all over the place, and posters of people I didn't recognize. They all had beards. You could tell right away that this was a house where no parents lived.

Stevie took me into the kitchen. A boy was sitting at the table, drinking a cup of tea. "Hi," he said to me.

"Hi," I said back. He had a very nice smile and sleepy eyes. His hair was blond and silky.

"My name is Michel," he said, and that was when I realized that he had a French accent.

"I'm Becca," I said. "Stevie's sister."

"Oh, I know all about you," he said. "Stevie's been talking about you all week."

I felt pleased and embarrassed. "Sit down, Becca," Stevie said, and I sat across from Michel at the table. "How's an omelet?" asked Stevie.

"Fine," I said.

Stevie went to the counter and cracked eggs into a blue bowl. Then he made me a perfect omelet, with tomatoes and cheese. "See?" he said. "This is what happens when Mom isn't around to cook for you. You learn how to do it yourself. No Spaghetti Os for me."

The omelet tasted wonderful. Stevie sat down at the table, and the three of us began to talk. Michel's voice sounded like a song when he spoke. He was from Quebec, he told me. He worked with American draft resisters in Canada, helping them get set up and find jobs. He was nineteen, too.

When I finished eating, I began to realize how exhausted I was from the trip. Stevie took me upstairs and showed me where I would sleep. I could have his room, he said, and he would sleep downstairs on the couch. His room here looked exactly like his old one—very neat, as usual. His guitar was lying across the bed.

"Do you still play it a lot?" I asked.

"Yes," he said. "As a matter of fact, I've been jamming with two guys at work. We're thinking of starting another band."

"What will you call it?" I asked.

"Caribou," he said. "I still like that name best of all."

"Have you ever seen a caribou?" I asked Stevie.

"Only in pictures," he said. "But they're very pretty. They run fast, too. I read that they're going extinct. They're a very gentle animal—like Bambi."

Before I went to sleep that night, Stevie sat down on the edge of the bed and played me a song he had written. It was all about being far away from home. His voice sounded even better than ever. He closed his eyes and had a dreamy expression on his face.

When he was done singing, he got up and stood at the door, holding his guitar. "Well," he said, "I'll see you early in the morning."

"Stevie?" I said.

"Yeah?" he asked.

"This is the best trip I ever went on."

"It's barely started," he said, but he smiled.

The next day we went on a whirlwind tour of the city. There were a lot of hills to walk, and my feet hurt. But there were wonderful things to see. Many of the buildings were old and had big green domes instead of regular roofs. A lot of people talked French.

We went and had lunch at the restaurant of a big, fancy hotel.

"My treat," said Stevie. "I have a little extra cash."

We sat outside, on a terrace overlooking a lake. There were paddleboats on the water—a red one, a green one, and a white one. People stood by the railing and took photographs. It was very peaceful.

"So tell me things," I said.

"What do you want to know?" asked Stevie. "A lot has happened since I left, Becca. I don't know what to say."

"Do you get homesick a lot?" I asked.

He didn't answer for a second. "Yeah," he finally said. "Sometimes it gets pretty bad. I get stoned a lot—too much, I think. We get the munchies and eat whole boxes of these things that look like Twinkies but have a French name."

I was shocked. I thought about the drug film we had seen in school and the way that girl had stared at her hands and started to freak out. I didn't say anything, though. I just looked down at my plate.

"Things are hard," Stevie said. "You make me out to be this perfect brother, but I'm not, Becca. I get stoned, and I just goof around a lot. I don't know what I'm going to do with my life yet. I really have no idea. I'm turning into a loner or something."

"What about a family?" I asked. "Don't you miss being part of a family?"

"Of course I do," said Stevie. "But it's not as easy as all that. I mean, our family has turned out to be a disappointment. At least, that's the way I see it. Maybe you're too young to understand what I mean."

I looked out over the water. I wasn't too young. I knew what he meant. I imagined my mother and father in the kitchen of our house. I thought about my dad, sitting at the table with a newspaper in front of him, and my mom, just standing at the stove with a faraway expression on her face. I never really knew what she was thinking.

Maybe they didn't understand me, but I didn't understand them either. It *was* a disappointing family in a way. My parents wouldn't accept a lot of things, wouldn't even listen. But then I began to think about all the people who *would* listen to me. I began to think about my favorite counselor, Jessie, and how happy I had been that summer. How even though I had been homesick at first, I had ended up crying when camp ended in August. I thought about Kate and her parents, and I thought about Stevie and me on a family vacation in Miami Beach. We had stayed in a motel and had stayed up late putting quarters in the machine that made the bed vibrate. It was supposed to relax you, that machine, but it just made us laugh. Dad kept knocking on the door that connected our room with theirs and told us that we'd better "pipe down."

Stevie had made it easy for me when we were growing up. Now he was gone, "in exile," like he said, and I had been feeling sorry for him. What about me, though? Wasn't I in exile, too, living in the house with just Mom and Dad? It was hard being the only kid. I knew what Kate went through. I suddenly missed her very badly. I loved Stevie, but Kate was the only person I could really tell *everything* to.

You got different things from different people, I realized. Your parents took care of you, but if they didn't understand you, then you had your brother or your best friend. And that was the way life worked. You kept finding people you liked, and you spent a lot of time with them.

My brother and I sat together in the sun, not talking. I felt happy and sad at the same time. It was like reading a wonderful book—you love it while you're reading it, but you also feel upset because you know that it's going to end soon. You don't know what to feel.

That night Stevie and his housemates and I all went out for a pizza. I finally met the other guys Stevie lived with. Matthew was tall and skinny and serious, and Daniel was round and funny. They were like a comedy team. I looked across the table at Michel and watched him picking up a slice of pizza in his long, pale hands. If I met someone like Michel in junior high school, I could fall in love in a second. I wondered what the boys would be like in junior high school.

In the van, driving back from dinner, Michel put on a rock station, and we all sang along, even me, who has a terrible voice and didn't know most of the words. It was okay, though. Nobody seemed to mind.

Nothing big happened while I was in Canada. Stevie and I stayed up late every night, talking. I told him about school, and the mural, and all the trouble I had gotten into.

"Wow," said Stevie. "You're a little rebel. You'll probably be joining me in Canada in a few years, when they start to draft girls."

Sometimes, I thought, Stevie didn't take me all that seriously. He made me feel like a little kid. But maybe that would change as I got older. When we were both completely grown-up, the seven years between us wouldn't make a difference at all. We would just be like regular friends.

The week was soon over. It hadn't been nearly enough time. "In junior high school," I said, "I'm going to try to win every contest they ever have. I'm going to save up all my money and come and visit you again."

The morning I went back home, the weather was perfect. I said goodbye to Matthew and Daniel and Michel, and they all hugged me like old friends. I couldn't wait to tell Kate about Michel. He had held my hand for a second before I left, and his skin was as soft as my own.

Stevie and I had breakfast in an International House of Pancakes. "I can't believe they have them here," I said. "I thought they only did in the U.S."

"*International*," said Stevie. "That's the key word."

We shared a tall stack of chocolate chip pancakes, but we weren't really hungry. I didn't want to go; it was as simple as that.

At the bus station, standing and waiting with me by the curb, my brother reached into the pocket of his jeans. "I have something for you," he said.

"What is it?" I asked.

"A present," he said, and he handed me a gift, wrapped in white tissue paper. It was very small. I stood there in the warm morning light and opened it. Inside was a tiny statue, carved of some sort of bone. It was a statue of a man. I loved it immediately. The bone felt very smooth under my hands.

"What's it made of?" I asked. "It's beautiful."

Stevie looked at me, and his dark eyes were serious. "Caribou," he said. "Since it's going extinct, you're not supposed to bring anything made of caribou out of the country. But I wanted you to have it. It's primitive art, very old. You can put it on your desk at home and think about me once in a while, if you're not too busy with junior high and boys and all that."

I held the little sculpture in the palm of my hand. This was the best present anyone had ever given me. The bus driver climbed onto the bus and started the engine. Then he stepped back down to collect tickets. The bus stood there, trembling.

"Oh, Stevie, I'm going to miss you so much," I said. "It isn't fair."

He pressed me close to him, close against his sweat shirt, which still smelled of incense. "You're a great kid, Becca," he said. "I get depressed up here. I wash dishes all night. I have my friends, but you—well, it's just different." His voice was low.

So I got on the bus, and the tears were running down my face hard now. I tucked the caribou sculpture deep in the bottom of my purse, underneath the postcards I had bought for Kate. I took a seat by the window, and no one came and sat next to me. I was glad; I just wanted to be alone and not talk to anybody. My head was filled with thoughts. Stevie stood at the curb and waved, and

I knew that saying goodbye to him now was probably the hardest thing I had ever done.

The bus pulled away, and Stevie was still waving. I turned from the window finally and leaned back against my seat. In a couple of hours we would reach the Canada–U.S. border. An American customs official would come onto the bus and make sure we weren't smugglers. But I would be smuggling out a piece of caribou. I was just a twelve-year-old girl, traveling alone. They would never suspect me of anything.

In a way it felt very dangerous. Stevie had given me something, and it was illegal for me to have it. But in a way it was also like I was taking a small piece of Stevie home with me.

I reached into my purse and touched the sculpture, felt its smooth edges with my fingers. I thought of who I had just left behind: my brother, my favorite person in the world. And I thought about what I would be returning to: Kate, and my room, and Skipper, and soon the beginning of junior high, and eight new classes. It was kind of exciting.

Maybe the caribou would bring me luck. I would carry it around with me everywhere in junior high school. I would put it in my locker during gym class. And maybe, I thought, someday it would bring Stevie home to me.

ABOUT THE AUTHOR

MEG WOLITZER was born in 1959. She attended Smith College and Brown University, from which she was graduated in 1981. She is the author of the adult novel *Sleepwalking*, which *The New York Times* called "lucid, insightful, and, most of all, tempered with the hard-won wisdom of compassion." She lives in New York City.

Special Offer
Buy a Bantam Book
for only 50¢.

Now you can order the exciting books you've been wanting to read straight from Bantam's latest listing of hundreds of titles. *And* this special offer gives you the opportunity to purchase a Bantam book for only 50¢. Here's how:

By ordering any five books at the regular price per order, you can also choose any other single book listed (up to $4.95 value) for only 50¢. Some restrictions do apply, so for further details send for Bantam's listing of titles today.

Just send us your name and address and we'll send you Bantam Book's SHOP AT HOME CATALOG!